Skye Without Limits

by

K.M. Daughters

Sisters of the Legend, Book 3

This is a work of fiction. Names, characters, places, and incidents are either the product of the author's imagination or are used fictitiously, and any resemblance to actual persons living or dead, business establishments, events, or locales, is entirely coincidental.

Skye Without Limits

COPYRIGHT © 2022 by K.M. Daughters

Cover Art by *Kim Mendoza*

The Wild Rose Press, Inc.
PO Box 708
Adams Basin, NY 14410-0708
Visit us at www.thewildrosepress.com

Publishing History
First Edition, 2022
Trade Paperback ISBN 978-1-5092-4142-2
Digital ISBN 978-1-5092-4143-9

Sisters of the Legend, Book 3
Published in the United States of America

The door at the rear of the room closed with a loud boom. Skye turned around at the rude interruption. Her heart somersaulted.

Summer leaned toward her. "Who is that cutie?" She waggled her eyebrows. "Please sit next to me."

"That's Gabe."

"Gabe? Your Gabe?" Summer nudged Bree in the ribs and gave a head nod in Gabe's direction.

"Oh, my goodness," Bree said. "He's a serious hunk, Skye."

"What is he doing here?" Skye wracked her brain for any mention Gabe might have made that his full schedule included attending hearings on this all-important issue.

He's on the Energy and Resources Committee? I really should pay more attention.

Her spirits soared. Surely the man she loved was her most powerful ally in this battle. He knew how deeply she cared about marine life. Now she couldn't wait to continue making her case.

"Please accept my apologies for the interruption," Gabe said striding to the head table with a young woman scurrying behind him. "Traffic."

He and his assistant took the two empty seats at the head table. Skye's eyes remained glued to his handsome face. Her confidence that she might succeed in her mission grew with Gabe in the room.

"Folks, this is Senator Gabriel Hartley," Governor Jordan said. "We just started the meeting, Senator. Miss Layton, please continue."

Gabe's focus snapped to Skye's position on the podium. His eyes met hers and a sexy smile curled his lips. "Miss Layton, you have my full attention."

Praise for K.M. Daughters:

Bewitching Breeze, Book 1, Sisters of the Legend: "If you're looking to be swept away on the wings of love with a dash of the mystical thrown in, pick up Bewitching Breeze today. I can't wait for the next book in the series."

~*~

Only One Summer: "Well done, K.M. Daughters on building a solid mystery wrapped in a fantasy romance. Even though this is book two, it can be read as a standalone. Highly recommend!"

~*~

Awards: The Carolyn Readers' Choice Award, Bewitching Breeze; International Digital Award, Reunion For The First Time; Booksellers' Best Award, Fill The Stadium; Bean Pot Award, All's Fair In Love and Law; The Lories Best Published, Beyond The Code of Conduct and Against Doctor's Orders

Dedication

For Our Children. Being your mother fills our lives with endless magic. Thank you with all our love.

Acknowledgments

Thank you always, Ally Robertson for your expert editing and your sweet, loving manner. It is pure pleasure working with you. Thank you to Joelle Walker and Nicola Martinez, our first and much-loved editors. You, and everyone at The Wild Rose Press, have made our published author dreams a reality. Our love and gratitude to our husbands and children and grandchildren for being avid fans and for providing us endless inspiration and encouragement. And more than anything, we are grateful for our sisterhood and our beautiful parents who gave us each other and everything.

Prologue

Outer Banks, North Carolina 1918
The Legend Of The Three Butterflies

Madelina Binder Sullivan slept fitfully that night as she had every night since her darling husband, John, had shipped out to join the Allied Forces in Europe. Worries about the burden of responsibilities she shouldered in his absence plagued her during every waking moment and persisted in her subconscious throughout each night. Would she keep her infant, triplet daughters content without their beloved father? Could she maintain the Inn of the Three Butterflies alone and safeguard her family's livelihood? And even while successfully managing without him, how would she not perish from loneliness?

Her sisters Lottie and Beth lived so far away from the Outer Banks, and her parents had taken up residence outside Washington, devoted to the war efforts. Her mother's visions, quietly imparted to her military veteran father, now a consultant at the Pentagon, helped develop troop strategy. Lina Sullivan was proud of her family and grateful to the Sacred Source for the noble use of the powerful gifts that flowed strong through the Binders' generations. Each night before bed, her prayers were full of gratitude for past and future blessings. But sound sleep eluded her in the empty, four-poster bed.

Tossing and turning, she dreamed that a spinning, alien sun had descended upon the inn devouring the rafters like kindling. Choking, acrid fumes filled her lungs. Gagging she awoke, her eyes instantly stinging and streaming tears from the black smoke that poured from beneath her bedroom door, up to and along the ceiling, tumbling waves of poison.

Terror threatened to take hold of her, but she refused to allow panic to seize her despite the unbreathable air and the sure knowledge that roaring flames awaited her escape through the door. Her babies lay in their bassinet in the next room. Lina calmly assessed her means to reach them.

Her gaze lit on the window. She bolted out of bed and raced to the window side of her room. Hellfire reflections of the blaze undulated in the glass. She took hold of the bottom of the sash, thrust upward, and rattled open the window. A din of crackling, spitting pops and the clang of the fire brigade nearing the inn sounded in her ears. She leaned out the window. The sill pressed uncomfortably into her midriff as she twisted her torso to take full measure of the window in the babies' room. Lina exhaled in relief at no visible sign of tendrils of smoke curling out from the window frame.

Closing her eyes, Lina bound the spell, prepared to take flight and divebomb the neighboring window with her pelican beak. A flurry of movement in the corner of her eye in the next instant told her that she had only moments to execute her plan. The fire brigade was seconds away from the inn.

She swooped off the sill into the silky, humid air and flew a distance of one hundred feet away from the building, reversed her trajectory and then flapped her wings, mustering every ounce of power in flight and abandoning any thought of self-preservation. Her single focus was to save her daughters.

Lina thrust her beak through the glass barrier as if spearing the crests of waves diving for fish. She crashed through the girls' bedroom window and sprawled limp on the oval rug in front of their bassinet.

The Sacred Source blessed her with sufficient power to transform and then crawl toward her children. She grasped the edge of the bassinet and dragged herself up to a kneeling position to peer inside the bed before she collapsed on the floor.

Three red butterflies flitted over their mother's face as if kissing her and then flew out the window and over the head of the fireman who perched on the top rung of the ladder.

Chapter 1

Present Day, Outer Banks, North Carolina

Skye Binder Layton needed to pack for her trip to California—now. But she wanted to linger in her studio and finish painting the scene that intruded in her mind no matter what else demanded her attention. She couldn't resist drifting over to the canvas, picking up a brush and abandoning her open suitcase. Skye had already showered; had dressed in her customary pastel print maxiskirt, a fitted tunic, and sandals; had applied light makeup; and had pinned up her waist-length, auburn hair.

Her underwear and toiletries were packed. As for the rest, how much time could it take to figure out what she'd pack to wear for eight days combined in the desert and on the southern California coast? No problem.

Her Maid of Honor gown awaited her arrival in the Palm Springs Bridal Shop, so that necessary wardrobe piece was out of her hands. She had crated her paintings and shipped them to the La Jolla and Newport Beach galleries. Skye could spare a few minutes to finish the painting.

She dipped the brush into a dollop of tangerine acrylic paint on her pallet and then swept the brush on the canvas adding slashes of color to the inferno that dominated the scene. Lost in her art, Skye focused on the images in her mind. Her right hand wielding the brush connected with her vision as if she opened a valve to let creation flow.

"Well, that's interesting." Mike Layton's hearty baritone coming from close behind her gave her a start and had her nearly smearing the brush stroke.

Skye turned around and faced her father who was clean shaven even at three A.M. and smelled of Old Spice aftershave, the scent of Dad to Skye's family. "You like it?"

"I do." He moved closer to the canvas. "It's the fire at the original inn, isn't it?"

"Uh huh." She paced over to the sink, turned on both faucets, and tested the water temperature with her left hand. Rinsing the bristles of the brush under the flow of lukewarm water she continued, "I don't know why I needed to paint it. Maybe the new print run of The Legend brochures that arrived a couple days ago inspired me. I think it's amazing that Great-Great Grandma Lina survived after rescuing Great Grandma and her sisters."

Mike chuckled. "There's a *lot* that's amazing about The Legend. Those fantasy"—Mike made air quotes with his fingers—"brochures entertain our guests no end. If they only knew."

He turned away from the easel and surveyed her open suitcase. "We need to leave in fifteen minutes for the airport. Doesn't look like you're anywhere near ready. Want me to see if Mom will lend you a hand? She's up already to see you off."

"Nah." Skye waved away his suggestion. "I'll get my act together. See you downstairs in less than fifteen minutes."

"Okay, sweetheart."

Her physically imposing, but teddy bear father lumbered out of the room. Skye strode into her walk-in closet and studied her wardrobe assessing her clothes for suitability for the trip. She slipped four sundresses off hangers, plucked a couple pairs of strappy sandal flats out of the shoe organizer bins, and unclipped several maxiskirts from skirt hangers. Her arms full, she transferred the clothes to the daybed where she had spread open her suitcase. Skye rapidly folded the clothes and neatly packed them.

Next, she rummaged inside her bottom dresser drawer and drew out three pairs of shorts and tank tops. She closed the drawer and opened the next one up in her bureau where she kept her collection of swimsuits. Having lived in the inn on the Atlantic Ocean beach her entire life, except for the four years she had attended the prestigious Art Institute on the mainland, Skye owned bathing suits to spare. She dumped everything on the bed and returned to the bureau for work-out clothes and socks. One more trip to the closet for her "good" athletic shoes as opposed to the several pairs of sand-scuffed sneakers kept perpetually on the back screened porch, she was ready to pack the last of her things.

She latched shut the clasps on the suitcase, hoisted it off the bed upright onto the floor and unfurled the telescopic handle. Skye placed her hand on top of the handle and stood rooted to the spot listening to the thunder of waves pounding against the shore and gazing out her wall of windows at the inky outlines of clouds along the barely visible horizon. The magnetic hold her world here exerted on her arrested her and made her long to skip this trip—any trip—and remain where she belonged. Every creature beneath the water's surface called to her. She yearned to answer the call, take flight out her window and then, maybe plunge into the ocean for a swim.

Obligation to her best friend, and a genuine desire to see Lynn again after too much time apart, spurred her out her bedroom door and downstairs to meet Dad for the ride to the airport.

****

When Mike parked the Jeep at the curb in front of the terminal at Norfolk International Airport a couple hours later, Skye was downright weepy at the prospect of leaving. She wasn't accustomed to walking away from her loved ones. Her identical sisters often walked away from her with their comings and goings to the Inn of the Three Butterflies. Bree lived in Chicago and Summer lived in New Jersey, so get-togethers were few and parting always resulted in cryfests. For the first time since she had kissed Mike and her mom, Kay goodbye as a freshman college student, Skye appreciated that leaving was *way* harder than staying behind.

Mike set her suitcase down on the sidewalk and swung shut the cargo door of the Jeep. He swept her into a warm enveloping hug. Skye closed her eyes grateful for the loving father who unconditionally adored her, her sisters, and her mom.

He gently cupped her shoulders and held her at arms' length. "Be safe, sweetheart. Have a wonderful time at the wedding, and good luck with your gallery shows. Say hello to your Aunt Karol for me."

"I will, Dad," she choked out. "See you in eight

days." *I can't wait.*

Commissions on her work had steadily increased lately. Skye didn't suffer the slightest pang of guilt splurging on first class seats for the approximate seven hours of flight time with one stop in Denver into Palm Springs International Airport. She happily accepted the offer of a mimosa before takeoff and settled into the leather seat relishing the extra space in the forward cabin.

Several movies she hadn't seen were possible entertainment options on the plane. She had tucked a new Lee Child novel, her sketch pad, and charcoal pencils in her carry-on. Skye hoped the time aboard planes would…fly. If all else failed, she might try to nap. The time zone difference made it three hours earlier at her destination. She didn't want to fall asleep too soon that night and disappoint Lynn.

****

Skye filed off the plane, along the jetway, and into the gate area in Palm Springs International Airport. Her gait hitched until she worked the stiffness out of her legs. She swept through the automatic doors leading to the promenade to the baggage claim building. A furnace blast of superheated air fanned her body. Squinting in the bright sunshine, she absorbed the vista: a ring of reddish, jagged mountain peaks loomed ahead; an impossibly blue sky dotted with puffy, crystalline white clouds looked too perfect to be real; and several hummingbirds darted among the bougainvillea trees that lined the promenade.

The pilot had announced at landing that the temperature in Palm Springs was one hundred five degrees. Strange that Skye didn't perspire hurrying in the heat to meet Lynn. Instead, tension in her body loosened as if relaxing in a sauna. Shot through with anticipation of a joyful reunion, Skye stepped into the slowly revolving door and entered the building that housed baggage carousels and rental car counters.

Lynn waved an arm overhead from behind a velvet rope. Skye rushed over to her and threw her arms around her. She clung to Lynn and rocked back and forth a few seconds, squeezing her in a heartfelt hug.

Skye linked arms with Lynn and began walking toward the baggage claim area. "It's so good to see you. Are you nervous about the wedding? When do I get to meet Mark?"

Lynn beamed. "I'm more excited than nervous…so far. You'll meet Mark this evening at dinner. His mom is hosting a welcome reception for the out of towners at the Club. Be prepared to be wowed."

"By Mark or by the club?"

"Both." Lynn narrowed her eyes and gazed up at the electronic boards above each baggage carousel. "You're on three. How many bags did you check?"

"Just one large Pullman. It's bright red paisley. Can't miss it."

A strident buzz sounded, and the light flashed on claim area three as the conveyor belt jerked to a start with a mechanical groan. Skye retrieved her luggage and rolled the bag out into the shimmering heat in the parking lot.

Seated in the passenger seat of Lynn's comfortable SUV, Skye angled the air conditioner vents to fan her face, sighing with pleasure at the wafting cool air. "What's the plan for this afternoon?"

Lynn paid the parking fee at the booth and steered

out of the lot. "First, we need to stop at the dress shop so you can try on your gown. If it needs any alterations, the seamstress told me that she can have it ready for us tomorrow. Then, we can settle in at the house I rented for us. I have a light lunch in the fridge, and I thought we can go for a swim afterward. We have a private pool at this house. Did you bring your suit?"

"I did. Sounds great. But why did you rent a house? I thought we'd stay at your mom's house."

"She offered, but my aunts and uncles need a place to stay, and she only has three rooms for guests. I found our rental house through Vacation Palm Springs. It's pretty, and we have it all to ourselves."

"Can I at least go half with you on the cost?"

Lynn gave Skye a wave of her hand. "Don't be silly. It's nothing. Here's the dress shop."

Skye left the car and followed Lynn into the store. Lynn shook hands with a pert, blonde woman. "Hi, Susan. This is Skye Layton, my Maid of Honor."

Susan extended her hand to Skye. "Great to meet you." She gave Skye's hand a shake. "I have your gown hanging in the dressing room. Please come with me."

She walked briskly down a narrow hallway. "Would either of you like a glass of champagne?" Susan tossed out over her shoulder.

"No, thank you," Skye said.

"Me neither, Susan. Skye, I'll wait on that love seat." Lynn pointed to the mid-century vintage sofa positioned in front of floor to ceiling tri-fold mirrors.

Skye entered the dressing room. Susan closed the door behind her leaving Skye alone to try on the gown which hung on an ornate bar on the dressing room's wall. Skye fingered the Hunter green, satiny material, pleased that the dress was even prettier in person. She kicked off her sandals, shed her skirt and tunic, unzipped the dress, slipped it off the hanger, and stepped into the gown slipping the straps up over her shoulders.

Susan tapped lightly on the door. "I have your shoes, Skye."

"Come in."

"Here, let me." Susan put down the shoe box and stepped behind Skye. She zipped up the dress and fastened the hook and eye at the middle of Skye's back. "Ooh, this looks perfect on you. Try on the shoes. I don't think you'll even need it hemmed."

Skye opened the shoe box and slipped on each of the peau de soie pumps. The three-inch heels comfortably fit her and gave her just enough height for the skirt of the gown to skim the top of her feet.

Susan flung open the door. "Let's go show the bride."

Skye paraded down the hallway toward the mirrors, runway style, a little knock-kneed, hips swaying. She halted in front of the mirror grinning at Lynn's reflection. "What do you think?"

"I think you look amazing," Lynn enthused. "The color is perfect with your red hair."

She gazed at her reflection in the pretty, dark green dress that fitted to her narrow waist, and framed the emerald pendant that she wore in the vee of her bodice. Skye dressed up rarely, the last time five months ago at Bree's wedding. Usually, she felt uncomfortable in formal dress, but this gown looked formal, yet wore like a night gown. "Thank you, Lynn. I really love this dress."

Lynn turned her gaze toward Susan. "It doesn't need a thing."

Susan clapped her hands lightly. "Great. We'll press it, along with your gown, Lynn, and it will be ready for you tomorrow morning."

Lynn rose from the love seat. "Good. We'll see you then."

Back in the car, Skye enjoyed sightseeing. Lynn drove up a steep lane and then a steeper driveway and cut the engine. "This is it."

Skye bounded out of the car, eyeing the façade of the earth-tone stone, tiled roof ranch house with interest. "Pretty."

"Wait until you see the view from the pool."

She unloaded her suitcase and carry-on from the trunk, and then followed Lynn through the front door. Lovely air conditioning hummed, and the marble tiled floor cooled her feet through her thin sandals. Skye sighed, enjoying the welcoming atmosphere and the surprising spaciousness inside which she hadn't expected viewing the home from the curb. "Where should I put my luggage?"

Lynn pointed to her left. "We have identical suites on each side of the house. Go make yourself at home, and I'll put out some food. Would you like a glass of wine?"

"Oh yes, thank you."

"Chardonnay good?"

"Perfect."

Skye rolled her luggage into the bedroom. The inviting king-sized bed and overstuffed chaise in the corner of the room were luxurious. The walk-in closet was far more than she needed and the double sink vanity, huge soaking tub, and two-person shower made her uncomfortably aware that she had no special man in her life—had never had any man in her life to share a private oasis like that room.

She unpacked and hung the clothes that might wrinkle on hangers in the closet and then changed into shorts and a tank top. Meandering barefoot into the living room, she sped up to beat Lynn, who was overladen with a tray of food and wine glasses, to the sliding door leading to the patio. Skye slid the door open for Lynn and then followed her outside.

An overhead ceiling fan stirred the oven-like air. The jets in the full-size, rectangular swimming pool frothed the crystalline water. A semi-circle of mountain peaks sprawled in the near and far distance. The new vista entranced Skye, and she snapped photos on her phone rapid-fire to capture the natural majesty around her.

Lynn sat at the table, scraping a neighboring wrought iron chair along the Spanish tile floor nearer to her and then propped up both her legs on it. She held out a full wine goblet, dewy with condensation in Skye's direction. "Sláinte."

Skye joined her at the table and picked up the other glass of wine from the tray. She clinked her glass against Lynn's. "Sláinte. I'm so happy for you, Lynn."

Lynn took a sip of Chardonnay peering over the rim of her glass at Skye. "Thank you, sweetie. I'm so happy to see you. How long has it been anyway?"

"Gee. I've lost track. Maybe when you came to my first gallery show in Norfolk?"

"Right. Wasn't that like six *years* ago?"

"That sounds about right. I'm sorry, Lynn. I must

make more of an effort. I promise I will."

Lynn chuckled. "No, you won't. I know you too well, and it takes something big, like holy matrimony, to pry you away from your beloved sand bar. I love you dearly anyway. Thank you for being here for me."

Skye swept her arm in an arc. "Are you kidding? Look at this place! Thank *you*. Are you sure I can't chip in for the rental cost?"

"No, really. It is so good to just chill, isn't it?"

Skye huffed a laugh. "Is this chilling? Phew." She mopped her brow with her hand. "More like baking."

"Gets even hotter than this every June, July, and August."

"Well, I'm even more glad that I'm here in May, then." The ceiling fan didn't even approximate the caressing sensation of ocean breezes at home that Skye loved. But already something about that desert valley compelled and held promise for her.

"So…" Lynn popped a morsel of cheddar cheese in her mouth and then washed it down with a sip of wine. "Mm, that's good. I'm starving. Help yourself."

Skye sampled the food. "So, you were about to say?"

"Yes. So, how's your love life?"

She shrugged her shoulders. "Non-existent as ever."

"Not interested in anyone? Maybe even casually?"

"Nope." Suddenly wistful, Skye rested her elbow on the table and propped her chin in her hand. Bree and Jack were ecstatic newlyweds. Summer and Vinnie were recently engaged and always gave her the impression that they couldn't keep their hands off each other. How could Skye not yearn for her sisters' happiness with men who unconditionally accepted their truth?

No matter how much I might want that brand of happiness, who could EVER accept my truth?

She shook off the negative attitude. Skye loved her life and had no reason to complain. "I haven't met the right man yet, that's all. Speaking of...I can't wait to meet Mark."

"You will in a couple hours." Lynn rose from her seat and stripped her cover-up off over her head revealing a trim, black, low cut bathing suit. "Go get your suit on and let's go for a swim."

Chapter 2

After a luxurious dip in the pool, Skye stripped off her wet bathing suit, hung it on the bathroom's heated towel bar, and then wrapped herself in the provided terry cloth robe. She sprawled out on the bed intending to rest for a few minutes. Two hours later, gentle tapping on her door roused her from a deep doze.

"Skye, are you ready?"

Skye bolted off the bed and flung open the door. "I'm so sorry, Lynn. I fell asleep."

"It's okay. We still have plenty of time before dinner."

"Thank goodness. You look amazing," Skye said. "I'm afraid I'm going to be seriously underdressed for this dinner. Want to give me some advice on what to wear?"

Lynn followed Skye into the closet. "You'll look beautiful no matter what you wear." She appraised with a critical eye Skye's maxiskirt-dominated wardrobe hanging on the central rod. "But, since we always borrow each other's clothes when we're together, you're welcome to check out my closet."

Lynn fingered a multi-color skirt overlaid with lace. "Can I borrow this one for dinner tomorrow?"

Skye threw her arms around Lynn and squeezed her into a warm hug. "This is fun, Lynn. I've missed you so much."

****

Skye clipped a crystal encrusted barrette into her hair, fastening her curls up behind her ear on the left side of her face. She stepped back and gazed into the full-length mirror. The borrowed, peach colored dress with a scalloped hemline flattered her figure. The silky material hugged her bodice, waist, and hips, and belled at her knees.

She layered bracelets on her wrists, each one having special meaning to her, and then sauntered back and forth a couple turns practicing walking in the narrow-heeled, strappy beige sandals, also borrowed from Lynn. Skye put on lipstick, slipped her cell phone into a pearl clutch purse, and then hurried into the spacious living room feeling pretty and almost ready for the social demands of the evening.

"Wow, Skye. That dress looks *way* better on you than it ever did on me. You can keep it. I love your lipstick. What brand and color is it? I *need* it." Lynn chuckled as she plucked her car keys off the countertop. She led Skye to the garage. "It's just like old times, isn't it? You're so lucky to have sisters to share clothes and makeup shades and everything."

"I'm so thankful for my sisters, but they're not home much anymore."

Skye opened the car door and climbed into the passenger seat as Lynn got into the SUV on the driver's side. "Besides, Bree and Summer wouldn't be caught dead in my clothes," she said on a laugh.

During the ride, Skye filled Lynn in on Bree's wedding and Summer's engagement.

"You're next." Lynn turned down a long driveway flanked by colonnades of fan palm trees.

"I highly doubt that." Skye brushed off Lynn's prediction having always considered marriage outside the realm of possibility. No man could handle *all* of her.

She peered through the car windows at the opulent grounds. The imposing country club building seemed cut out of the granite mountain peaks that towered above the roof line. Groomed golf greens were visible to the left and right of the building. In the distance a golf cart wended along a narrow, rolling path. Posted signs warned, "Private". The entire scene screamed old money.

Lynn steered the car around a semi-circle and braked under the portico in front of the club house. "Welcome to my future in-laws' home away from home." Lynn snickered. "I don't think Mark's mother has cooked a single dinner in her own kitchen."

"Wow, Lynn." Skye grimaced, uncomfortable at the prospect of relating to such wealthy people. She wiggled her cramped toes in the dressy shoes and wished she was home on her beloved beach, barefoot and in shorts.

"I know that look." Lynn touched Skye's hand.

"What?"

"You always wore that expression on your face when you were about to disappear from a party because you thought that you didn't fit in." She squeezed Skye's icy hand. "You are a gorgeous, talented artist who is making a very nice—correction, insane—income. You belong wherever and with whomever you choose. I wish I could make you understand."

"You know me so well. I *am* trying to be more sociable. I promise I won't disappear tonight."

Someone yanked open the driver's door, and Lynn

jumped in her seat. "Oh, Mark, you scared me to death."

"I'm sorry, love, but I couldn't wait another minute." Lynn's fiancé dipped his head inside the car and planted a kiss on Lynn's lips.

The valet opened Skye's door. She accepted the young man's handhold and stood on the paver-stone path leading to the club's oak double doors waiting for Lynn and Mark.

Mark draped his arm around Lynn's shoulder and shepherded her toward Skye.

"This is Mark Remington, Skye," Lynn said, her eyes shining. "Mark, Skye Layton, my best friend in the world."

Mark released Lynn and gave Skye a hug. "It's great to finally meet you. Lynn has told me so much about you; I feel like I know you already."

"I feel the same way, Mark." Skye gazed at Lynn and her man.

The pictures Lynn had sent didn't do him justice. Mark was Brad Pitt handsome, and Skye could easily see Lynn's attraction to him. But the contagious smile that lit his entire face surely had captured her best friend's heart the most.

"Let's go inside. People can't wait to meet Lynn's Maid of Honor, the famous artist."

"Oh, Lynn. You didn't tell people that did you?"

"Of course not. Mark, stop teasing." Lynn playfully slapped his arm.

"I'm not teasing. We didn't have to tell the guests anything but your name, Skye."

Skye's nervousness increased anticipating a socially torturous evening. She wanted commercial success for her work and was thrilled she had gained some measure of recognition in the art world. If only she didn't have to mingle…

"I think I need a drink," Skye said.

"I'm pretty sure that can be arranged." Mark stepped in between Skye and Lynn and gallantly crooked his elbows.

Skye and Lynn hooked their arms through his and sashayed through the double doors held open by *two* tuxedoed gentlemen. They waited near the door of the elegant ballroom while Mark headed to one of many bars on the perimeter of the room for their drinks.

Hundreds of people milled around tables covered in black linen. Enormous centerpieces of fully bloomed white roses monopolized the center of the tabletops. One entire wall was open-air, providing a jaw-dropping mountain view. A soft, flower scented breeze set scores of candles around the room flickering.

Lynn pointed straight ahead. "There's Mom and Dad. Let's go say hello."

Skye allowed Lynn to gently tow her forward toward her parents.

Lynn's mom squealed. She zipped toward Skye and enfolded her in a lovely hug. "Skye, you look wonderful."

"So do you, Mrs. Proctor. It's so good to see you."

"No more Mrs. Proctor. It's about time you called me Debbie."

"And call me Wayne, honey," Lynn's dad said.

"Hi…" Skye hesitated unused to the familiarity. "…Wayne."

Debbie took her hand. "Come on, sweetie. Let me introduce you to Mark's parents and friends."

Skye and Lynn kept pace with Debbie crossing the ballroom toward a group of five people.

"Amelia and Brad, this is Skye, Lynn's sister of the heart."

Brad Remington extended his hand. "I'm delighted to meet you, Skye." He gave her hand a light shake. "I read an article about you in Southwest Art Magazine. Your work is intriguing."

"Thank you for the compliment." Skye blushed, still unused to popularity. She gazed at Mark's mother. "And thank you for inviting me to dinner this evening."

Skye turned her attention to the other three people in the group.

"Where are my manners?" Amelia Remington said. "These are our good friends, Savannah and Gene and their daughter, Sharon."

"Nice to meet you." Skye exchanged handshakes with the trio, relieved that she didn't have to make small talk since Lynn monopolized the conversation discussing wedding details.

"Finally, here comes Mark with our drinks," Lynn said.

Mark wound through the crowd trailed by a strikingly handsome man.

"Do you know that man behind Mark?' Skye whispered to Lynn.

Mark handed Lynn her drink distracting her.

The gorgeous stranger swept Skye into his arms and fused his lips to hers in stunning, breath-robbing intimacy. The world stopped turning. She should have shoved him away and ended the inexplicable assault. But she froze, saw starbursts behind her closed eyelids, her bones seemingly melting. Skye had never experienced this ignition of desire. She was muddled and shaken when he ended the kiss. But all she wanted was to draw him back toward her for more.

"Darling, there you are," he boomed. "I hope you don't mind if I steal her away," he said to the group at large.

He trained long-lashed, chocolate brown eyes on Skye's face as if interested only in her out of all the women in the room…or on the planet. "I want to show you off to some of my friends here."

Skye's head spun. She glanced at Lynn. Her friend's furrowed brow told her that she had no ready explanation, either. Realization dawned on her. *He thinks I'm one of my sisters.* Which one, Bree or Summer, might that captivating man have *ever* called, "darling"? Probably Summer.

Before she could utter a word, he clasped her hand and steered her outside. He didn't stop until they reached the bar.

"I need a drink. Would you like one?"

She nodded. "Champagne."

He ordered her drink and a beer for him while he still held her hand.

The bartender handed a flute to Skye and a pilsner to him. "Sit with me a minute so I can explain?" He pointed to a bench facing the mountain range.

"Sure." Still clasping his warm hand, she strolled over to the bench and sat down next to him.

He gulped some beer. "I'm sorry for accosting you. You must think I'm nuts."

Skye huffed a laugh. "Actually, I don't. It's happened to me before."

He arched his eyebrows. *"Really?"*

"You'd be surprised how often." She pursed her lips, disappointed that she wasn't either of her sisters. "Do you know Bree, or probably Summer?"

He looked at her like she had spoken in a foreign language. "Who are they?"

"My two identical sisters...I thought...you didn't mistake me for either of them?"

He wagged his head no.

Indignation surged through her. "Then what the hell *was* that?"

"I'm sorry. I saw Sharon standing there and I... reacted." He took another swig of beer. "Mark didn't tell me she'd be here."

"You have a problem with Sharon?"

"Well, sort of. We were engaged. She wasn't faithful. I broke the engagement. I *have* moved on. But then I saw her, and all I thought was I'm going to kiss the most beautiful woman in the room and make Sharon believe that she was my lady. Make her jealous. Or regretful. Admitting this, I sound completely insane. Again, I'm very sorry."

Skye gazed at him. His curly, longish black hair framed the fair-skinned, perfect Celtic features of his face. The five o'clock shadow shading his jawline emphasized his chiseled chin and Black Irish handsomeness. His piercing brown eyes searched her eyes, perhaps begging her forgiveness.

If he could read her mind, he'd know that she not only didn't mind his kissing her one bit, but also that she was delighted he hadn't mistaken her for anyone else. *The most beautiful woman in the room...my lady...huh.*

"What the hell, Gabe?" Lynn stomped over to the

bench, her hands on her hips.

"In my defense, Mark didn't tell me Sharon would be here. I was blindsided."

"Wait. So, you attack my best friend, engage in a giant PDA in front of everybody we know, and then whisk her out here? What the hell were you thinking?"

"Obviously, I reacted without giving it much thought. I've already apologized to the lady."

"Yeah, well, great…"

Skye burst out laughing. She faced him. "Gabe, is it? At least I know your name now."

Lynn rolled her eyes. "Good grief you didn't even introduce yourself?

"Skye, this is Gabriel Hartley, Mark's college roommate and best friend."

Skye grinned widely and offered her hand to him. "Good to meet you, Gabriel."

A grin curled on his lips. He turned her hand over and kissed her palm. "And who is this beautiful woman?" he asked Lynn, gazing into Skye's eyes.

"This is Skye Layton, my dearest friend. Take your hands off her."

"Nice to meet you, Skye." He ignored Lynn and clasped Skye's hand tightly, a wicked, magnetic gleam in his eye.

"I have to get back inside. Are you coming, Skye?"

Skye was perfectly content gazing into Gabe's soft eyes. "I'll be there in a little bit, Lynn."

Lynn huffed a breath, spun on her heel, and headed back into the ballroom.

Gabe slipped his hand away, draped his arm behind Skye's back, and cupped her shoulder with his large warm hand.

She relaxed within the comfortable shelter of his arm as if she had known him a long, sweet time. The mountainside directly in the forefront of her view glowed golden from up-lighting along the base of the cliff. The air smelled sweet. Skye closed her eyes and took a deep breath. She hadn't anticipated the evening's entrancement.

"This is my first visit here. I didn't expect the lushness and beauty in the desert. Do you live here, Gabriel?"

"No, I visit here often to see Mark. I live on the East Coast."

"Really? I do, too. Where do you live?"

"Virginia."

"I live in Nags Head."

"No kidding. I have a cottage in Nags Head."

The maître d' appeared on the patio. "I need the Maid of Honor and Best Man to take their seats, please."

Skye and Gabe hopped up from the bench at the same time.

"Are you kidding me?" She beamed at him.

"You see?" he said. "We're meant to be together."

Skye held his hand entering the ballroom. When she reached the middle of the room, she stopped, stood on tiptoes, and kissed his cheek. "Just in case Sharon is watching."

Chapter 3

Skye awoke in the shadowy room. Her body clock had yet to regulate from east coast time, and the sun hadn't risen yet. She stretched her arms overhead and then brought the tip of her index finger to her lips where the memory of his kiss lingered. *The* kiss.

Her astonishing first encounter last evening with Gabriel had left an indelible mark on Skye's heart. And throughout the rest of the night, his interest in her seemingly hadn't waned. She had sensed the heat of his gaze on her several times during dinner. When Skye had glanced in his direction, Gabriel had winked or waggled his eyebrows at her, his brown eyes dancing.

The last thing that Skye had anticipated embarking on the trip to Palm Springs was looking forward to the wedding tomorrow with pulse revving anticipation. She looked forward to whatever Lynn had planned for today, too. Skye couldn't stop smiling.

She slipped out of bed and tiptoed into the kitchen to brew a pot of coffee, hoping the machine wouldn't hiss a racket and wake Lynn. Skye filled a mug, padded through the living room to the sliding glass door, eased the door open, stepped outside onto the patio, and set her coffee cup down on the glass tabletop. Wrapping a pool towel around her shoulders to stave off the early morning chill, she snuggled into the cushions on a chaise lounge, sipping coffee and gazing at the interesting cloud formations over the mountains.

Peace and wonder filled her spirit, and she mused on the similarities between her attraction to the beach and now, the mountains. Her mind pleasantly blanked waiting for dawn and for Lynn's companionship, content and loose-limbed.

The sun fully breached the horizon, and Lynn still hadn't emerged from her bedroom. Skye dispensed with the beach towel she had cocooned in, the temperature having rapidly climbed. She wandered over to the small pool, tested the water with her toe, squatted to sit down on the paver-stone rim, and then plunged her feet into the swirling foam. The jets kneaded the backs of her calves. She enjoyed the spa-like pleasure dangling her feet in the cool water until she heard rumblings from behind her.

Skye twisted around to face the glass door. Lynn came out onto the patio clad in a white cotton nightshirt. "Morning, sweetie."

"Morning, Skye. Did you sleep well?"

"Complete lights out the minute I hit the pillow until about an hour or so ago. Amazing."

She couldn't remember the last time she had a dreamless slumber or a seven-hour block of time, awake or asleep, without impressions or visions or the Layton sisters' singular ESP invading her consciousness. Unusual, certainly. But yesterday *was* a long day. Perhaps exhaustion explained the phenomenon.

Lynn sat at the table, fueled on coffee, and quietly fiddled with her cell phone while Skye enjoyed doing nothing.

When Lynn apparently hit her caffeine limit, her social director persona emerged. "I'd like to go for a jog for an hour or so. Want to come with me?"

"Sure."

"And then we need to shower and dress for a casual dinner."

Skye knit her brows. "After we finish jogging? Won't that be at around nine in the morning if we leave now?"

Lynn glanced at her phone's screen. "Maybe more like nine-thirty," she said. "But we'll be out all day. I made early dinner reservations at Miro's for us. It's my favorite restaurant and having dinner there is my idea of the perfect bachelorette party. After we eat, I thought we'd stroll the Street Fair. They close a large section of Palm Canyon Drive for local artists' and vendors' booths, produce markets, and food carts. It's fun, if you're up for it."

"Whatever you want. Thanks for planning all this. My treat for dinner. There's no way I'll let you pay for your own party."

"Deal," Lynn said. "Thank you. First thing, we'll pick up our dresses and then bring them to the Brides' Room at Our Lady Of Solitude. Then I thought we'd visit the Art Museum downtown. The curated collection is fantastic, heavy on mid-century Modernism. There's an exhibition of California desert landscape paintings that I think will fascinate you. Also, some masterworks on loan from a private collection of Impressionist and Abstract paintings. Then, I thought we'd go to the Museum satellite in Palm Desert, if we have time, to view the inaugural Art Council exhibit of local artists' works. I figured you wouldn't want to miss either place. Who knows when you'll come back?"

Skye swung her feet out of the water and sat on the

edge of the pool. "Oh wow, the whole day sounds terrific. I'll go change my clothes."

Skye fell into an easy rhythm jogging with Lynn. Her muscle memory kicked in from their running mate days during college. She followed Lynn's lead down the incline from the rental house and winding through the Old Las Palmas neighborhood of Spanish style mega mansions and offbeat mid-century revivals. Lynn rattled off a litany of the celebrities who had lived in the estates they passed: Dinah Shore, Liberace, Kirk Douglas, Ann Miller, Mary Martin, William Powell, Edward G. Robinson, Gene Autry, Jack Warner, Samuel Goldwyn, Elizabeth Taylor, and Debbie Reynolds.

Lynn pointed to a gated property taking up an entire block. "Mark's parents live there."

Skye widened her eyes. "No kidding. How rich do you have to be to afford a place like that?"

"Ha! I never asked for the bottom line, but I think inheritance on his mom's side has a lot to do with their lifestyle. Mark is way more normal working as a lawyer, thank God."

"Did Mark and Gabriel go to undergrad or law school together?"

Lynn nudged her shoulder. "I was wondering when you'd get around to pumping me for information about Gabe."

"I'm not…"

"Of course, you are, and why not? I don't know why I never thought of it before—you two make a great couple. I take it you've forgiven him for making that spectacle with you last night?"

Skye grinned. "There was nothing to forgive." She

fanned her face with her hand. "Lord that man can kiss."

Lynn giggled. "I can only imagine. Did he explain himself, at least?"

"Yes. He was trying to make Sharon jealous by kissing, and I quote, 'the most beautiful woman in the room.' "

"No question you fit the description."

"Oh, Lynn." Skye said. "You're biased."

"Not at all. You know, you and Gabe have a lot in common."

"Really? What?"

"You're both gorgeous, and you're the only ones who don't know it."

"He *is* seriously gorgeous. And he didn't strike me as cocky at all. So, what's his connection with Mark?"

"They went to UVA together, both undergrad and law school. They were freshmen roommates by chance and were fast friends since. Like you and me."

Skye touched Lynn's bouncing shoulder. "I don't know what I'd do without you."

"Same for me. No matter how infrequently we see each other, we still stay connected."

"Always."

"Haven't you heard the name Gabriel Hartley before? Maybe in the news?"

Skye frowned. "I don't think so."

"Gabe is the wunderkind, conservative Junior Senator from Virginia. His name has been mentioned as a possible Presidential candidate for the Republican party after this administration ends."

"I've honestly never heard of him before. But I'm not much of a news-watcher. And I purposely avoid politics."

"I'm with you there. But Gabe isn't your average politician. He really cares and is determined to use his office to make a difference. It sounds sappy, but he's the real deal. Mark kind of hero worships him now."

"So, what's the deal with Sharon?"

"Good question. We were worried about Gabe after he broke the engagement. I wonder if he succeeded last night in making her jealous. The guy who caused their break-up is history. She didn't bring a date last night and isn't bringing a plus-one to the wedding, either."

Skye crested a hill and reversed to loop back at Lynn's side. "Gabriel said that he's moved on. What do you think?"

"Absolutely. It isn't about wounded pride, though. He can't trust her, and that's everything."

Every impression and detail about Gabriel that Lynn had shared affirmed Skye's instincts that he was a special man. She had the deepest sense that meeting him, even under the extraordinary circumstances, signified a momentous beginning for her. She was even more excited now about the upcoming wedding.

****

It was pure heaven entering the cool house after their jog. Skye headed directly to her bathroom. She stripped off her sweaty clothes and draped them over the lip of the bathtub to dry. Stepping into the huge shower, she stood beneath the pulsing spray. More pure heaven. She washed quickly even though she could have enjoyed the refreshing shower until the hot water ran cold.

She tucked a towel around her and walked into her bedroom. At the door, she hollered,

"Lynn, what do you want me to wear?"

Lynn appeared outside her bedroom door. "Any one of your sundresses or long skirts and flat sandals would be perfect. It shouldn't be too crazy hot for walking at the Street Fair tonight. I call dibs on that lace skirt."

"I'll bring it over to you."

By eleven o'clock Lynn and Skye had swung by the Bridal Shoppe, put down both back seats in the SUV, and loaded two long dress bags lengthwise into the trunk.

Lynn took Skye on a short drive and parked outside the quaint, Spanish Mission style church where the wedding ceremony would take place the next day.

Skye balanced her dress bag over her arms and followed Lynn inside the hushed chapel that smelled like furniture polish and candle wax, down the center aisle, and through a door to the far left of the altar. They hung their gowns in the room where they'd dress tomorrow and then returned to the car bound for the Museum.

****

"Oh Lynn, come over here and look at this one."

Lynn ambled over and stood shoulder to shoulder with Skye in front of the oil painting. "Glorious."

Skye gazed at the work, lost in the artist's eagle's nest perspective of an array of mountain peaks bisected and encompassed by charcoal clouds. "I swear, the cloud formations I saw this morning looked exactly like this. I love this painting."

"I knew you would. It's my favorite in the entire museum."

Skye wagged her head. "We really are soul sisters,

aren't we?"

She lingered a few more moments in front of the painting and then shuffled around the gallery viewing more of the Plein Air Landscape Artists exhibit. "Do you still paint, Lynn?"

"Rarely. Occasionally a friend or relative will commission something. I do my work almost entirely on the computer, even freehand drawing and painting. I'm doing some photography now, too. Photoshop is a miracle invention."

"It is, and I'm all thumbs with it. I'm still very old school. Do you miss working at an easel?"

"I don't. But I know it's different for you. Your work is breathtaking, Skye. Really. How do you do it?"

"I'm not sure how to answer. What do you mean?"

"Well, for instance, that pelican series you did. I swear I thought that bird would fly off the canvas right into my face."

Skye shrugged. "Thanks. But I just paint what I see in my mind. Inside. It's hard to explain. Basically, if I couldn't paint, I couldn't breathe."

"Yes. I know that about you." Lynn wrapped an arm around Skye's shoulder. "Feel like walking through a sculpture garden?"

"I'm not sure. How hot is it out there?"

"Maybe ninety. But it's dry heat."

"Oh. Like ninety degrees in an oven rather than in a steam bath?"

Lynn snorted. "Yep."

"I think I'll pass. What are my other options?"

"How about a glass of wine in a nice, air-conditioned bar before we go to dinner?"

"Now you're talking."

"There's only one catch."

"Oh yeah? What's that?"

"The bar is four blocks away, and we'll never find a better parking space than the one we have across the street from here. It's best if we walk."

Skye burst out laughing. "You're killing me, Lynn. Let's go."

Chapter 4

Gabe and Mark sat at a corner table on the clubhouse patio. A waiter placed a platter of wings in the center of their table between two half-full pilsners of beer. Gabe ordered another round and then piled some wings on his plate.

"This is the life." Mark drained his beer glass. He leaned back in his chair.

"It sure is." A welcome breeze ruffled the damp hair at the nape of Gabe's neck. "I can't remember the last time I could spend a day golfing with no phone calls or interruptions. This is exactly the kind of bachelor party I want, too."

"Are you trying to tell me something?" Mark arched his eyebrows.

On a laugh, Gabe shook his head. "Absolutely not. Since taking office I've become a monk."

Mark snorted. "You expect me to believe that?"

"Believe it or not, it's true." He gazed at the clouds shadowing the mountain and mused about Sharon's betrayal, pleasantly surprised that thoughts of her no longer brought pain.

"Having any regrets?"

Gabe picked up on Mark's concern over the state of his dormant love life. Dealing with heartbreak had challenged Gabe, especially when campaigning without his future wife by his side. But he had bested political opponents, had put Sharon behind him, and hadn't looked back.

"Thanks for caring, but you can stop worrying. I'm good. And I love my work. I'm grateful that Grandpa lived long enough to see me sworn in. Ever since he retired from the Senate, he plotted to have me carry on the public service tradition. He was my most ardent campaigner, even more than Mom. I couldn't let him down. It's still hard to believe he's gone. Last month his attorney gathered the family and read his Will. He left me the OBX beach cottage. Do you believe it? He knew how much I loved being there with him."

"I remember the graduation party he threw for us at the cottage." Mark laughed. "I don't know who drank more beer. I think, maybe him."

"Definitely him." Gabe grinned. "You and Lynn have to come to the beach when you can get away and we'll lift a glass in his memory."

"Deal."

"Now, what would you like to do on your last night of freedom? I found a strip club called the Oasis in the Desert about a half hour away. How does that sound?"

Mark grimaced. "Sounds awful."

"Okay. I'm up for anything. What would you rather do?" Gabe finished the last wing on the platter. "Actually, I wouldn't mind staying here all night."

Mark leaned toward Gabe and propped his elbows on his knees, his eyes sparkling. "Let's go crash Lynn's bachelorette party."

"Really? Are there male strippers involved?"

He huffed a laugh. "Not her style. She's having dinner with Skye at our favorite restaurant."

Gabe's heart skipped a beat at the mention of Skye's name. He would like nothing better than to spend time with the woman he could not stop thinking about, had even dreamed about last night. Guilt pinched at the memory of his rash lip-lock with the unsuspecting woman, who thankfully wasn't outraged at the assault. Quite the opposite. Skye had returned his kiss in memorable surrender. "If you're sure that's what you want, I'm in."

He checked his watch. "It's 4:30. What time is their reservation?"

"I think early. I'll call Miro for details and let him know we'll join the ladies. He's our friend who owns the restaurant."

"Perfect. I'll settle up here and meet you at the car."

****

In Mark's condo, they separated to shower and change. Gabe enjoyed the hot water spray pounding his back but couldn't spare the time to linger. He turned off the taps and wrapped a towel around his waist. With a few sweeps of his hand, he wiped condensation off the mirror and then raked his fingers through the black hair curling below his ears. He slid his phone off the marble countertop surrounding the sink and set a reminder to schedule a haircut next week.

In his bedroom, he tucked a crisp, linen, black and white pinstriped shirt into snug black jeans, shoved his wallet and cellphone into his back and side pockets and then joined Mark in the living room.

Gabe enjoyed the car ride down Palm Canyon Drive as Mark expertly drove around the tourists who haphazardly crossed the street.

"Do you like living here?" Gabe said.

"I do. But we don't live here permanently yet. I

have the condo in L.A. on the market. And I haven't fully moved my firm to the desert. I might keep the office in L.A. open anyway. Dad works part time at the office here. I could go back and forth as needed. It's only a two-hour drive. Lynn can work anywhere on her designs. We're building a house in La Quinta. It's time for us to put down roots."

"You're a lucky man."

"I am. And I'm thankful every day." He steered into a parking slot in front of Miro's Restaurant and switched off the engine. "There's Lynn's car."

Gabe unfurled his long legs out of the car and followed Mark through the open door of the red brick and white stucco building. He assumed that the man who gave Mark a bear hug was the owner.

"Good to see you." The Slavic accent confirmed the man's identity as Miro.

Miro trained his brown eyes on Gabe. "And this must be your friend, Senator Gabriel Hartley."

"It is. Gabe, this is Miro Terzic," Mark said.

"Nice to meet you."

"Welcome to Miro's. So glad you could come tonight. I have a special bottle of wine breathing on the ladies' table." He ushered them into the main dining room through an archway and led them to a table for four in the back corner of the restaurant.

Lynn squealed with delight and jumped up from her seat as Gabe and Mark approached her.

"I can't believe you're here! Your ears must be ringing. We were just talking about the two of you." Lynn wrapped her arms around Mark's waist and stood on tiptoes to peck his lips.

Mark grinned down at her. "That's nice to hear. I

couldn't stay away. I hope you don't mind our joining you?"

"Are you kidding? I'm thrilled."

Skye shoved back her chair from the table and rose to greet them. Her napkin fell off her lap. Gabe stooped to pick it up. In the same moment Skye squatted down. Gabe barely avoided knocking heads with her, their lips a breath away from each other. He read the invitation in her eyes and kissed her soft lips.

"Hey! What are you doing down there?" Lynn lifted the edge of the tablecloth.

Skye stiffened, jerked away from him, and stood upright. "I dropped my napkin. We...went for it at the same time."

Her gaze met his. Skye's jade eyes glimmered with mischief, and a pretty blush pinkened her porcelain skin.

This woman...

Gabe took the seat at the table next to Skye relishing her nearness and the sweet floral scent of her perfume. A waiter poured the wine, and they clinked each glass in turn toasting Lynn and Mark.

"How was your day?" Mark hung his arm over Lynn's chairback.

"It was wonderful." Lynn leaned toward him. "We did all our errands, and I even had time to show Skye the art museum."

Gabe turned toward Skye. "Are you interested in art, too?"

She pursed her lips. "You could say that."

Lynn hooted a laugh. "Do you two get out much?"

"What do you mean?" Gabe said.

"First, Skye had no clue that you, Gabe, are an in-the-news Senator. And how is it possible that you have never heard of Skye Layton, the freaking famous artist? Do you people read newsfeeds at all?"

"I'm sorry." Gabe gazed into Skye's eyes. "I don't know much about the contemporary art world, and lately I haven't had time for anything other than work."

"No need to apologize to me. I'm sorry, too. I never watch the news. Politics makes me crazy."

Mark chuckled. "Well, aren't you two the perfect match?" He accepted the menu the waiter handed him.

"Maybe we are," Gabe murmured.

****

I think maybe we are, too. Skye widened her eyes at Lynn and then buried her face in the menu.

"What should I order?" Gabe said. "Everything looks good."

"We always start with an order of cabbage rolls," Mark said. "Lynn orders sesame crusted tuna with red pepper sauce, even though it's not on the menu. Miro knows how much Lynn loves the dish, so he always orders tuna fresh for her. I either have the beef stroganoff or the rack of lamb. They're both equally delicious."

"One time he actually flipped a coin." Lynn giggled.

"Maybe Skye and I should order one of each and share." Gabe touched Skye's arm. The gentle contact sent a surge of pleasure through her.

"No, thank you. I'd like the lentil Bolognese." She handed the menu to the waiter.

"Rack of lamb for me, please," Gabe said. "Medium." Gabe leaned closer to her. "If you change your mind, you can sample my dinner."

"Actually, I'm a vegan. Since I was five."

"Really? You decided that young to forego meat?" Gabe handed his menu to the waiter and gazed into Skye's eyes.

She held his gaze, warmed by the lively interest in his coffee-colored eyes. "I did. According to my mom I was adamant about it and insisted, Momma, no more meat for me."

Skye only vaguely remembered the declaration, but vividly remembered the motivation. At age five, she discovered her ability to transform into animals which irrevocably changed her point of view.

"Obviously, you were a very advanced kid." Gabe's broad smile revealed white, perfectly straight teeth and dimpled his cheeks—absolutely arresting.

"I'm devoted to animal protection."

"I admire that," Gabe said.

The waiter served dinner—Skye loved her meal— and the wine flowed. The conversation and laughter at the table increased in volume as Mark and Gabe shared some of their college antics. Skye had never felt this open and free in a man's company, accustomed to a lifetime avoiding vulnerability to safeguard family secrets. Gabe inspired something new and radically different in her. Trust? Maybe. Gazing at his handsome face, she hoped she could trust him.

Skye didn't want the evening to end, so she was delighted when Gabe and Mark seized on Lynn's invitation to the Street Fair.

****

The balmy evening was perfect for wandering outdoors. Mark and Lynn linked hands and strolled along Palm Canyon drive in front of Gabe and Skye.

Vendor stalls lined about ten blocks of the main thoroughfare in downtown Palm Springs, closed to traffic once a week, year-round, for the Street Fair. Gabe reached for Skye's hand and threaded his fingers through hers, happy that she clasped his hand gently.

"Pretty night," he said.

"Yes. I've discovered that I really love the desert." She spoke in a near whisper—a sweet, soft inflection that begged his full attention. There was a calmness about her that magnetized him. She hadn't known who he was—something that hadn't happened to him in social circles for a long time. No pretense. No ego. No female ambitions for his political future. Gabe could just...*be* with her.

"I plan on coming back. The sky and the clouds look different here. I could go on and on about the changing views of the mountains. The cactus, the hummingbirds... Oh, and the adorable roadrunners. The desert creatures are all calling to me to paint them." She stopped talking abruptly. "I'm sorry."

"For what?" He drew her to a halt facing him.

"I sound obsessed."

"No, you don't. I think you're utterly adorable." He tipped a finger under her chin tilting her lips upward so that he could kiss her, taste her sweetness. She nibbled on his bottom lip, and his heart swelled. *Lord, I want her.*

Drawing away he gazed deeply into her shining green eyes. "You're beautiful."

"Ah, *amore*." A strolling accordion player launched into a rendition of *O Sole Mio*.

Gabe twirled her in a pirouette and then drew her into his arms swaying with the music. A group of people clustered around them and clapped when the song ended. Gabe bowed and Skye curtsied. He wrapped his arm around her shoulders and hurried to catch up with Lynn and Mark.

"Do you have hollow legs?" Skye quipped as Gabe stood on the line at a cart selling kettle corn moments after he finished eating a double ice cream cone. "If I hadn't sat next to you at dinner, I'd swear you didn't eat a thing today."

Gabe shrugged his shoulders. "I burn through food fast." He held the buttery-sweet-smelling bag of popcorn out in front of her. She grinned at him with a playful glint in her eyes and scooped out a handful.

The foursome walked the length of the Street Fair and back, drifting from booth to booth and occasionally stopping to chat with a vendor about artisan items and desert-grown produce.

****

Skye snuggled next to him in the back seat of Mark's car. As Mark pulled into the lot in front of Miro's Restaurant and parked in the space next to Lynn's car, Gabe leaned over and kissed her cheek. "Thank you for a lovely evening."

She faced him, her emerald eyes sparkling. "Thank you. I had a great time." She cuddled closer gazing intensely at his mouth and then brushing a soft, butterfly-wings kiss on his lips that ignited sparks throughout his body. He resisted deepening the kiss and locking her in his arms lacking privacy. He had never wanted physical contact more.

Mark and Lynn opened their car doors prompting Gabe and Skye to break apart. Gabe rounded the rear bumper of Lynn's car and held open the door for Skye.

"I'll see you tomorrow. I claim the first dance."

Skye beamed at him. "I'll honor that claim. Good night, Gabriel."

Still grinning up at him, she climbed into Lynn's SUV, and he closed her door, his gaze locked on her face. Gabe didn't take his eyes off the retreating car until the taillights disappeared around a curve.

Chapter 5

Kay answered on the first ring, "Inn of the Three Butterflies."

Skye's heart warmed at the sweet sound of her mother's voice. "Hi, Mom."

"You're up early. A lot to do for the wedding?"

"Yes. But I have probably hours before hair and makeup. Lynn's sleeping now, and I guess I'm still on our time at home."

"Well, I'm glad you called. I miss you."

"Miss you, too. Have you..." Skye trailed off unsure where to take the conversation. *Have you seen anything, Mom? Have you seen him? Is he my future?*

"Have I what, darling?"

"Um, have you heard from Bree and Summer?"

"I have. They both have their airline tickets set. And they're looking forward to seeing you at the end of the month."

"Oh, me too. How's Dad? Everything good at the inn?"

"We're doing great. Have a wonderful time at the wedding, and I can't *wait* to hear about the showings. I'm so proud of you."

"Thanks, Ma. Talk to you soon. Love you."

"Love you, too, darling."

Skye ended the call, happy about connecting with her mother but dissatisfied that she hadn't consulted with her about Gabriel's sudden appearance and rapid prominence in her life. Skye hadn't "seen" anything, and if Mom had, she would have said something without prompting. Since neither Bree nor Summer had called Skye, she assumed the same for her sisters. She didn't know how to interpret that, except perhaps that her relationship with Gabriel hadn't really gelled yet. At least, not in reality. In her dreams, she and Gabriel had gone well beyond "gelling".

A soft tapping sounded.

"Lynn?" Skye said.

Lynn cracked open the door and peered at Skye. "I'm glad you're up. I couldn't sleep."

Skye moved over in the bed and patted the mattress next to her. "Come on in."

"Thanks." Lynn bounded over to the bed and stretched out next to Skye propping up against the headboard. "I'm a bundle of nerves."

"Seriously? You've seemed so calm. You're not having second thoughts, are you?"

"Oh no. I can't wait to marry Mark. I just want the whole down-the-aisle spotlight thing to be over."

Skye chuckled. "I'm with you there. But don't worry. You'll be the picture of grace. When do we have to start getting ready?"

"We have hours. Want to go for a jog? Maybe help me burn off some nervous energy?"

"Sure." Skye threw off the sheet and swung her legs over the side of the bed. "Let's go."

****

Skye gently wafted the long train on the white, tulle, beaded dress while Lynn's dad, Wayne held Skye's bouquet. She fussed with the folds of the fabric behind the bride until she was satisfied that Lynn's gown draped perfectly. "There. You look absolutely gorgeous."

She stepped in front of Lynn accepting the bouquet of sweet spring-scented white peonies and freesia from Wayne and faced forward in her first-place position in front of the arched oak doors at the entrance of the adobe church.

Skye looked over her shoulder at Lynn. "Ready?"

Lynn nodded.

"Okay," Skye said to the wedding director.

The doors swept open in front of Skye bringing the sounds of harp music and the rumble of guests shifting in the pews to gape at Skye standing in the open doorway at the back of the church. Gabriel's eyes held hers. He stood ramrod straight next to Mark on the right side of the central aisle, heartthrob handsome in a black tux and snow-white shirt. The intimate smile that spread across his lips and dimpled his cheeks spurred a flood of joy and anticipation through Skye. Her heart leaped as she stepped forward in cadence with strains of *Pachelbel Canon in D*. She floated down the aisle in a dreamy haze toward the man who increasingly seemed destined for her.

He didn't break the eye lock even when Skye halted to the left of the aisle across from him, and the bride made her entrance. The steady, sexy, loving expression in his soft eyes wildly complimented Skye. Gabriel made her feel desirable...powerful, and confident.

Lynn had opted for a ceremony versus a Mass: short and extremely sweet with a kiss to seal future happiness and a crescendo of applause from the family and guests in the picturesque, little church. Skye's heart swelled at the first organ chords of the Recessional hymn because next, she'd link arms with Gabriel Hartley and stroll up the aisle as a couple.

She slipped her fingers around his firm bicep, and he possessively covered her hand with his, sending electric rills of pleasure through her the entire way to the stretch limo idling at the curb in front of the church. Skye ducked her head, hunched over, and took a seat in the car facing Lynn and Mark. Gabriel athletically situated next to her for the fifteen-minute backward ride in the limo.

Mark popped the cork on a bottle of Dom Perignon champagne soaking up the fizz with a provided napkin. Gabriel held out four flutes one at a time for filling. Leaning forward in a squatting stance, the Maid of Honor and Best Man clinked glasses toasting the new Mr. and Mrs. Remington.

Skye's artist's eye delighted in the wedding reception venue—a 1920's mansion named "Little Camelot" that perched on a boulder-strewn hillside with 360-degree mountain and Coachella Valley views. Over one hundred olive trees and thirty palm trees forested the grounds. The rose garden's lush blooms provided gorgeous photo opportunities. Everywhere Skye turned she saw a canvas in waiting.

The photographer barked out, "over here…over there…move a little right or left," directions to the wedding party in his professional frenzy. Skye obediently posed this way and that, her jaws aching from wholly genuine smiling in Gabriel's company.

"How about the Maid of Honor and Best Man over here?" the photographer said.

Gabriel clasped her hand and led her over to the

designated spot. A pre-sunset, pinkening sky streaked with lemon-colored rays over the crests of mountain ridges provided the perfect backdrop. She turned to face the photographer. Gabriel wrapped his arm around her, his large, warm hand at her waist branding her as his.

I absolutely want this photo to frame. Skye had no difficulty beaming at the camera lens.

Finally released from posing, the wedding party strolled to the patio area to join the cocktail hour in progress. Lynn and Mark were supplied with flutes of champagne and began making the rounds greeting their guests.

Gabriel didn't let go of Skye's hand until they reached a waist high, linen draped cocktail table. "Would you like more champagne?"

"Actually, I'd like a Tequila Sunrise."

He laughed, a deep throated baritone. "I think tequila sounds just about right. Be right back."

****

She dispensed with the little umbrella in the drink that Gabriel brought her and took a long, satisfying sip. "Thank you. Delicious."

He clinked his glass against hers. "To Lynn's beautiful Maid of Honor. I'm so lucky to have had you on my arm."

Pleasure zipped through her at the compliment. "You make me blush, Gabe. Thank you."

"Only telling the truth."

"Did you always want to run for office, Gabriel?" she said.

He took a sip of his tequila with lime. "Yes and no. I majored in Poli-Sci and then went on for my law degree. I passed the Bar and thought I'd lawyer for a human rights advocacy firm. But politics is in the family blood. My maternal grandfather was a Senator— a damn good one if you ask me. And he nudged me in that direction. My mom more or less shoved me in that direction."

"Uh…was that a problem for you? What about your dad?" Skye thought of Kay and Mike fondly, appreciating that they never nudged or shoved—only supported.

"Not a big problem. Mom means well. My dad died when I was a kid. I try to remember how difficult it was for my mom to raise me alone, and I accept her doting for what it is—an expression of love. Truthfully, I thought when I tested the waters campaigning and found that I had a solid base of supporters, that being elected would allow me to do way more for human rights than in a law office. I hope at the end of the day that my record proves me right. But…"

He reached across the table and clasped each of her hands in his, warming her with his touch. "I'm tired of talking about me. I'm fascinated that you're an artist. Tell me…"

A loud chime sounded and a tuxedoed maître d'hôtel boomed, "Ladies and gentlemen, dinner is served in the rose garden tent."

Skye and Gabriel processed into the enormous tent toward the head table. The ornate centerpieces filled the air with fresh floral scents, and flickering candles on the tables spelled romance to Skye. She took the seat next to Lynn. Gabriel sat down to Mark's left. Suddenly feeling empty cut off from Gabriel, Skye pondered the serendipity of meeting him, and the happy fact that she had promised him the first dance.

But first, came the nerve-wracking prospect of proposing a toast in front of hundreds of people.

The disc jockey sashayed over to the table speaking into a handheld mic. "Attention, ladies and gentlemen. The Maid of Honor, Skye Layton, and the Best Man, Gabe Hartley will toast the Bride and Groom."

Her palms clammy, Skye rose plucking a full champagne flute off the table and holding it in her left hand. She accepted the mic from the DJ with her right hand. "Lynn and I became sisters of the heart the instant we met in a cramped, institutional ugly dorm room freshman year. The first thing we did together, after making our twin beds and stowing our belongings, was run to the art supply store for what we needed to paint an under-the-sea mural on every square inch of the drab walls in our room."

Lynn chuckled. "We were called to the Dean's office the second day of school."

"We were. And she immediately advised us in no uncertain terms to 'return the walls to their original eggshell white color.' But Lynn asserted that would be a grave mistake and requested that the Dean herself inspect the walls before enforcing her decision. Lynn argued, 'this is an art school after all.' So, the Dean visited our room. And the mural stayed."

"She couldn't believe her eyes. It was pretty magical," Lynn said. "Mostly because of Skye."

"Nah. We were in it together. The paintings are there in that dorm room now, I'm sure. We chose paint that lasts forever. Just like our sisterhood and the love my special Lynn shares with Mark—forever." Skye raised her glass. "Lynn and Mark, I wish you forever love, health, good fortune, and lots of magic. Cheers."

Relieved and satisfied that she had done her last duty at the wedding, Skye sank down in her seat and enjoyed Gabriel's humor and sexy physique in his perfectly fitted tux as he gave his toast to the bride and groom. His longish raven hair curled at the ends framing his heart shaped face. The five o'clock shadow that darkened his chiseled jawline had Skye contemplating how scratchy his beard would feel against her face when he kissed her. She couldn't wait for him to kiss her again.

"Slainté, Lynn and Mark. All happiness in your life together," he finished the toast.

Skye was served a lovely vegetable plate which she enjoyed while chatting occasionally with Lynn and listening to the love songs playing during dinner. After Lynn and Mark finished their meals, the DJ brought them to their feet to dance to… "Lady in Red"?

Lynn returned to her seat at the head table when the dance ended. Skye caught Lynn's eye. "Why that song?"

The bride hooted a laugh. "The first time we met I wore a red dress. Mark requested the song. I kinda love that he did."

"Yeah, me too."

Ed Sheeran's "Perfect" played next.

Gabriel came up behind Skye. He held out his hand. "I claim my dance now, Skye."

She gazed up at him and accepted the handhold. On the dance floor, he folded her into his arms, his large hand warming the small of her back. Skye nestled her cheek against his shoulder, closed her eyes, and placed her right hand lightly on his chest. He covered her fingers with his hand pressing them close to his heart. Gabriel led her in a floaty, sensual waltz across the dance floor, expertly rising and falling in the rhythm of the ballroom dance.

He twirled her out an armlength and then reeled her back into his arms, a lovely, graceful maneuver that hinted at his experience dancing. "You're a wonderful dancer, Gabriel."

"Thanks. No-choice lessons when I was a kid."

"Really? Me, too. But lessons were voluntary for me. All three of us took ballet and tap." A wave of fondness surged through Skye just talking about Bree and Summer.

"That's right; you mentioned you have two identical sisters. Wow. There are two more gorgeous yous. Your dad must own a big shotgun."

Skye giggled, his description 'gorgeous' delighting her. "Dad *is* protective. But there are no firearms at the inn as far as I know."

"The inn?"

"Yes. The Inn of the Three Butterflies on Nags Head Beach. Do you know it?"

"Absolutely. Your parents own it?"

"Uh huh. I live there. I work out of my studio on the top floor of the inn."

"Mermaid Cottage isn't too far from you down the beach."

"I know that cottage. Is it yours?"

"It is now. My grandfather died recently and left it to me."

"I'm so sorry."

"Thank you. I miss him."

The song ended and Gabriel released her from the

dance hold clasping both her hands. Linked together, they stood facing each other. Candlelight sparkled in his brown eyes and gleamed on his black hair. He gazed into her eyes, riveting her to the spot. He bent his elbows and drew her closer to whisper in her ear, "If we weren't on a crowded dance floor, I'd kiss you properly."

She tossed back her head and laughed. "Since when does a crowd stop you from kissing me?"

Skye arched her neck, stood on tiptoe, and kissed his lips softly. His arms locked around her pressing her breasts against his chest as he deepened the *very* properly executed kiss. The music started up again, shifting from romantic waltz to freestyle *Dancing Queen*. Still, he kissed her, igniting thrilling sensual tugs at her core and wanton lust: all new but irresistible sensations for Skye.

Gabriel loosened the embrace and gently withdrew his lips on an exhale. "Skye?" he said softly.

She stood immobile with him in the middle of the floor while dancers gyrated around them. "Yes?"

"I want…" He hesitated gazing down at her, his eyes hooded. "…to dance with you all night."

"Okay."

"Can I see you tomorrow? Let's spend the day together. I'll ask Mark and Lynn to recommend things to do."

She frowned. "I'm so sorry. I can't. I'm driving to the coast tomorrow. I have a gallery showing in La Jolla and another in Newport Beach before I fly back to Norfolk."

He sighed. "I'm disappointed."

Gabriel clasped her hands tightly. "Promise you'll

see me on OBX? I plan to use the cottage every chance I get."

"Of course. I'd like that."

"Come on." He tugged her gently into motion off the dance floor. "I'd like to give you my phone number, etc. May I have yours?"

She grinned from ear to ear. "Yes."

Chapter 6

Skye hopped out of the car parked near the departure doors at Palm Springs International Airport and then leaned her head back inside. "Thank you so much, Todd."

"You're more than welcome, miss." The driver met Skye at the back of the black Ford Explorer. He wrestled her heavy suitcase out of the rear cargo compartment and hoisted it onto the sidewalk, extending the telescopic handle. "Are you sure I can't help you inside?"

"No, thank you. I can manage from here." Skye shook his hand placing a folded twenty-dollar bill in his palm.

"Oh. Thank you very much," he acknowledged the tip. "It's a pleasure to meet you. I hope you'll visit us again."

"Definitely."

Skye followed the signs for rental cars in the baggage claim area and queued behind a toe-tapping impatient customer on the long snaking line leading to the counter. Apparently, planes had just landed. Good thing she wasn't in a hurry to get to her aunt's house. She planned to take her time along the scenic drive through the mountains on the way to the coast.

An hour later, Skye slid into the seat, started the engine, and immediately opened the convertible top. After battling her luggage into the car, she maneuvered the fire engine red Mazda Miata out of the lot. Her bulky suitcase occupied the passenger seat next to her because there was no way she could cram it into the car's tiny trunk. She had wrapped the seatbelt strap around the case and slid the buckle into the lock to anchor the bag.

The morning sun warmed her shoulders, and the wind batted her ponytail against her neck and OBX baseball cap. The Nav on her phone predicted a three-hour trip—a delicious time alone to savor an exhilarating drive along mountain and valley roads and relish unencumbered daydreaming about the gorgeous man in her life.

Her thoughts drifted back to the wedding. Lynn was the perfect bride. She and Mark had radiated pure love from the second their eyes locked at the church. Skye had never believed that she might find that soul mate kind of love for herself. Her prominence in the power of the Legend and the necessity to guard her secrets had prevented her from entertaining the possibility of marriage. Until Gabriel...

She had dreamed about him last night as she had every night since their explosive meeting, but the details of the dream remained murky. Skye was unsettled and edgy when she awoke that morning. Had they fought in the dream? They must have because she remembered telling him, "I'll never forgive you."

With a shake of her head, she blanked her mind, preferring to enjoy the songs on her playlist and leave her future, if there was a future for her with Gabriel, in the hands of the Sacred Source.

The trip took longer than the Nav's projection. Skye pulled over at every lookout point, grabbed her camera, and captured the top of the world views. At one stop, she turned around to head toward the car and startled at a pair of Bighorn sheep regarding her as if asking, who the hell are you? She loved the inquisitive expression on their faces and gleefully took several shots looking forward to painting them when she returned home to her studio.

"Get on with you, now," she said. "You're too close to the road here."

The animals immediately launched up the craggy hillside like aerialists, their coats blending with the mountain terrain in perfect camouflage.

At mid-afternoon Skye reached Karol's house. She drove through the open, massive iron gates fronting her aunt's mansion and parked on the circular drive directly in front of the cream stucco, red-tiled roof, hacienda-like building. Skye unbuckled her seatbelt, unclicked the lock on the passenger side that had secured her suitcase, opened her door, and stretched her stiff, long legs out of the car.

The front door flew open and her aunt, clad in a pastel caftan, ran barefooted down the steps. "You're here!"

Skye launched into Karol's outstretched arms for a hug.

"I'm so glad you're here, Skye."

"Oh, Aunt Karol, it's *so* good to see you."

Karol released the embrace, clasped Skye's hand, and drew her toward the house. "Leave your suitcase. John Paul will bring it to your room."

Movements in the doorway caught Skye's eye. Four Boston Terriers fixed cockeyed stares on her, their stocky bodies quivering with excitement.

"Who do we have here?" Skye crouched in front of the entry extending her hand, palm up.

"Yes, come meet Skye," Karol said in a sweet, conversational tone.

The little army pounced on Skye knocking her to her rear end on the paver brick driveway. Giggling she accepted a barrage of kisses. She sat on the ground swarmed by four wiggling bodies vying to sit on her lap at the same time.

Karol clapped her hands sharply. "Girls, behave yourselves. Please act like ladies."

Instantly the dogs obeyed their mistress and sat on their haunches in front of Skye in a straight row, casting her adoring, googly-eyed gazes.

"I'm in love." Skye laughed. She rose to her feet dusting off her skirt with her hands.

"John Paul." Her aunt's soft pronouncement of a man's name brought a blond Adonis dressed in white linen slacks and a pecs-and-biceps-grabbing, tangerine colored polo shirt, out through the doorway.

"Shoo." His direction to the terriers met with rapid response. Four wiggly hind ends disappeared inside the house.

John Paul extended his hand toward Skye. "It's great to finally meet you. Karol has talked nonstop about your coming for a visit."

Skye shook his hand and then he strode over to the Miata and hoisted her suitcase—which had represented back-breaking work to heave into the car for Skye—out of the car, as if the bag were as light as air.

Karol wrapped an arm around Skye's shoulder and drew her along behind John Paul into the house.

Skye halted abruptly, astonished at the home's

interior. The entire back wall straight ahead of her in the massive space was glass. Beyond the windowpanes the Pacific Ocean mirrored the azure, cloudless sky and provided a living mural.

"Wow, Aunt Karol. I don't have words. This is stunning."

"Thank you. I love it and I'll admit, it never gets old. With the push of a button, I can retract the windows."

"Really? Wow!"

"I still pinch myself every day. I can't believe I live here."

Skye drifted to the windows. In the yard, an inviting oval pool rimmed by lounge chairs with yellow-striped cushions situated to her right. A small ribbon of lawn off the pool deck bordered a sandy path that led to a rock hewn staircase. The beach below was lapped by gentle waves.

"I can't wait to walk on your beach in the morning."

"I love early morning beach walks every day. I thought right now you might settle in first, and then we can walk up to the cove trail to stretch your legs after the long drive."

"That sounds wonderful."

Karol led Skye up the impressive staircase, down a richly carpeted hallway, and into her guest room. The seafoam green walls and the huge bed covered with a white down comforter and heaped with assorted jewel-colored pillows made Skye feel at home.

An eight-by-ten easel frame on the bedside table drew Skye's attention. She picked it up and inspected the image. "I can't believe you still have this."

"Of course, I do. It's the first Skye original seagull. I figure if I save it a while longer, I can retire when I sell it." Karol regarded Skye pensively. "Actually, I doubt I'd *ever* sell my most treasured possession. I keep it in my bedroom and only moved it in here in honor of your first visit."

Skye gently set the framed painting down on the end table. "I was four when I painted it, but I remember that day vividly." She closed her eyes envisioning the past. "I sat on the deck growing more and more frustrated because I couldn't draw the seagull's eyes the way I wanted with crayons. And then you sat down next to me and gave me a tote filled with art supplies you had brought just for me. You gave me that canvas. And then you showed me how to place paint on the palette, explained how to mix colors, and handed me a brush. I'll never forget what you said."

"It's your turn to fly, Skye," she whispered. "You've soared ever since."

"I have you to thank for my career."

"Oh no you don't, darling. Your success in your career is entirely your own. I knew that your tiny crayon drawings displayed talent that would take you to great heights. I just gave you new tools."

"I'll always be thankful." She kissed Karol's cheek.

"Calling me your favorite aunt is all the thanks I need." She snorted a laugh. "Just to piss off your Aunt Kamille."

Karol patted her shoulder. "Go ahead and unpack or freshen up. When you're ready, we'll take that walk."

Skye washed her face in the guest suite's bathroom

and braided her hair into a long plait down her back. John Paul had unzipped and spread open her suitcase on a luggage rack in the room-sized closet. Eager to walk and explore, she delayed unpacking. Riffling through her clothing, she plucked out a peach-colored one-piece bathing suit, peach-gray striped linen shorts, and a pale gray peasant blouse. She stripped and dressed in the beachwear intending to go for a swim when she returned from the cove. With her sneakers and socks in hand, Skye went in search of her aunt.

Karol perched on the white leather sectional in the sprawling great room. Her aunt looked so much like her mother; she even dressed in Kay-like athletic clothes.

Skye trailed her up to the narrow La Jolla streets that led to the rock wall cove where seals and sea lions lolled in the sun. High above the ocean, the semi-circular path afforded a panorama of peacock blue sea and craggy promontories.

"Tell me about your young man."

Skye halted in her tracks at Karol's matter-of-fact statement. "You *see* him?"

"Maybe. Not identical to knowing that Bree and Summer fell in love. I saw a blossoming and then turbulence and confusion around you. Had to be a man." She arched her eyebrows, a wicked gleam in her eye.

"That's exactly how I feel right now. He…kind of entranced me. He's so handsome, Aunt Karol. And he seems to be just as taken with me. I've had dreams about him every night since we met...lovely dreams. But last night I think we were fighting in the dream. I don't know why. Maybe...." *He couldn't handle our truth.*

Skye gazed at the sea. "Can I ask you something personal?"

"Honey, you can ask me anything you want."

"Mom told me that you were in love once and you were engaged. Then the wedding was called off and you went to Greece to paint. What happened?"

"When James proposed I knew I *had* to tell him my truth. I dragged my feet during our whole courtship, and my sisters kept telling me that I had to reveal all before I could hope to have a life with him. They were right, of course. How could I hide my true nature from my supposed soul mate? If he truly loved me as I loved him, he'd accept all of me. He didn't."

Skye's heart cracked at the tears glimmering in Karol's eyes.

"The hardest part was the way he looked at me after I told him; like I was a freak. All these years since, I haven't trusted any man with my heart."

Skye and her aunt shared the same birthright powers. Would her aunt's experience predict Skye's future? "I'm so sorry." *For both of us.*

"Don't be. If I had it to do over again, I would. And truth be told, there is someone I might trust enough to love with all that I am. Right now, I'm taking my time. So don't let my story scare you off. James wasn't my soul mate. You'll know, just like your mom and Kamille and Bree and Summer knew, if you find the right man to trust. If you make a mistake of judgment like I did, just know that it's his loss and there is someone else waiting to accept you, all of you."

"Thank you. Gabriel was the Best Man at Lynn's wedding. He's so charming. I keep fantasizing about the possibility of marriage with him. Crazy. I've never even remotely thought like this before. Mom hasn't said a word about him. And my sisters haven't called, either. Do you see him in my future?"

"Not with any clarity, other than the sense that something powerful is going on with the two of you. That's not to say that he isn't the one. We're very much alike, honey. No one saw my fiancé coming or going. And no one knows about my new man." Karol winked. "Except you…"

Skye grimaced at a piercing pain in her arm. She rubbed the side of her triceps.

Karol knit her brows. "What's wrong?"

Skye squinted seaward focusing on movement in the stern of a motorboat bobbing at anchor encroaching on the protected waters in the cove. "I think a seal pup is in trouble out there."

Skye and Karol sprinted to the area on top of the sea wall where tourists clustered taking photos with cameras and smartphones. Dozens of seals and sea lions dotted the rocky points and sand below creating a din of barks and moaning screeches.

Scanning the area, Skye tuned in to the plaintive wail of a mother seal and pinpointed the pup floundering in a net tied to the stern of a motorboat. "There he is," she whispered. "You distract these people. I'll go."

Her aunt picked up on Skye's cue. "Oh my, look at those cute seals over there." She outstretched her arm and pointed away from Skye.

Skye distanced herself from the cluster of people before she jogged off the path and descended the sea wall's slippery rocks to the crescent of sand below. She bound the spell and simultaneously plunged into the icy water. Rocketing underwater she gathered speed and momentum until she collided broadsides with the boat. She leveraged the two hundred pounds of her sea lion's girth into the assault. The boat rocked perilously at impact dumping the three kids leaning over the stern onto their backsides. Skye dove deep under the vessel, unbound the spell, picked up a jagged piece of shell from the ocean floor, and broke the surface on the starboard side.

"Hey! Over here," she yelled.

A sandy-haired teen hauled himself up from the boat deck and peered down at her. "Where the hell did you come from?"

"Lifeguard stand," Skye improvised. "You were so busy breaking the law you didn't hear me on the bull horn? Or see me swim out here?"

"Uh."

"Untie your net and get out of here now."

He blinked, a deadpan expression on his face. "We're not leaving without our fish."

Skye treaded water casting him what she hoped was a threatening glare. "Think again. You know fishing is illegal in this area. My crew is on the way."

Sandy-hair mumbled something to his pals and minutes later, the trio untied the net and hung over the side of the boat glaring at her with passive aggression. Skye clasped the edge of the net as it hit the water and tugged the thrashing pup closer, detecting that the seal's flipper was tangled in the webbing. She doubted the shell shard would prove useful, so she let it slip between her fingers.

It's okay, little one. Calm down. I'll help you.

She continued to fan out the net, kicking her feet

furiously to stay above the surface, using the boat as a shield between her and onlookers ashore. Out of the corner of her eye, Skye saw a large gray seal slicing through the water toward her. *Here comes your momma. If you relax, I'll shake you free.*

Skye succeeded in loosening the net's hold just as the pup's protective mother swam between them. For one moment Skye faced the mother and heard her quiet thank you.

"You're so welcome," Skye whispered.

"Yay," came one of the kid's sarcasms. "Can we have our net back, lady?"

"Get out of here." Skye submerged and didn't turn around to see the kids' reaction to a huge red sea lion's wake on the other side of their boat. She approached the shore unworried about detection until she neared the shallows. Hitting the beachhead at the right spot was critical.

She decided not to unbind the spell until landfall. Skye waddled onto the beach and arched her sleek neck upward. If she moved as close as possible to the rock wall where she had come down, she could avoid detection.

Skye unbound the spell, scaled the seawall, jogged down the path until she caught sight of her aunt, and then strolled the rest of the way to Karol's left side.

"Oh, Skye, darling. You missed it!"

"You sure did," the man to Karol's right said. "A red sea lion came out of nowhere and banged into a boat out there. A little seal sort of flopped out of the net off the back of the boat, and a big gray seal swam with the little one over there." The guy pointed downward.

"Then the red sea lion appeared again and swam to

shore down there somewhere." He waved his finger in the general vicinity of the location.

"I have no idea how, but I swear that the red sea lion rescued that little seal." He shook his head. "I was so amazed that I forgot to take a single picture."

"Me too," a woman in a straw hat chimed in.

"I'm sorry you missed it, honey." Karol's eyes twinkled.

"Wow. Me too." Skye winked at her. "All I found was a broken shell. I threw it back. Wasn't much use."

Karol slid her arm around Skye's waist. "Come on. Let's go home. I'm pretty sure I have a big glass of wine with your name on it."

"Sounds perfect. I don't think I'll need that swim in the pool after all."

Skye and Karol strolled away from the still buzzing crowd.

Chapter 7

Gabe had hung on Skye's every word since they'd met and had committed to memory her plans the next few days. She had enticingly starred in his dreams and had him fantasizing about their next meeting. He wanted to know more about her—everything about her. Gabe wanted more Skye, period. His attraction to her was overwhelming, and he couldn't stop thinking about her. In fact, he didn't want to stop.

Was he impulsive to alter his plans to return home to Virginia after Mark began his honeymoon with Lynn? He shrugged his shoulders. Gabe's decisiveness had yet to fail him. Once he decided to travel to La Jolla, he fully committed.

"You can board now, Senator."

"Thanks." Gabe pushed through the private terminal door and met with a windy blast of dry hot air on the tarmac.

He climbed aboard the chartered helicopter, belted in, donned the noise cancelling earphones, and settled back in the leather seat. The blades overhead whoop-whooped and whirred, and the bird lifted from the helipad in stomach sinking pitch. Connecting to WIFI, he reviewed his emails and used every minute of the approximate hour flight to keep current on his responsibilities, only occasionally glancing through the window to appreciate the dizzying natural spectacle below and the bumper-to-bumper road conditions he avoided in the chopper.

A shiny black SUV with livery license plates idled twenty feet away from the arrival landing pad. The copter's rotary blades still swirled as Gabe exited the cabin, ducked low, and strode with his back arched toward the car.

The driver, wearing a black suit, white dress shirt, and black tie, popped out of the front seat and opened the passenger door just ahead of Gabe's arrival. "Sir," he said.

Tucked inside the limo, Gabe inhaled the pleasant new car smell. An array of that day's newspapers was stowed in one of the back seat pockets, a selection of that month's magazines in the other. He leaned sideways and thumbed through the magazines, plucking out a U.S. news journal. Flipping the pages, he noticed his name in print several times. Gabe still hadn't gotten used to the widespread reporting attached to him—thankfully, positive reporting since he took office.

Within a half hour, the driver reached the Bed and Breakfast in the village where an aide had reserved a room for him last evening. Gabe lifted his duffel out of the trunk in front of the white stucco building blanketed with climbing bougainvillea vines. His bag in hand, he ambled down a stone path lined on both sides by low hedges of fragrant, star-like jasmine blooms. He stopped in front of a wrought iron arch inhaling the flowers' aroma—the scent of Skye. Gabe considered the coincidence a very good sign.

Vivid memories of her played in his mind: her long, wavy auburn hair framing the porcelain skin of her face; the delicate blush that bloomed on her cheeks when he had kissed her first and each time after; the lush, sweet taste of her lips that left him ravenous for more; the electric silken sensation of her skin beneath his fingers that tempted him to explore every inch of her; the magnetic pull that her lawn green eyes exerted over him; the perfect features of her face and curves of her body; the way her smile illuminated her eyes entrancing him…

He had no idea when he had arrived in Palm Springs that he would leave thoroughly smitten by a woman.

Gabe opened the front door and entered the hotel encountering a plump, middle-aged man seated at a Victorian desk who welcomed him and invited him to take a seat on a chair opposite him. The self-described proprietor checked Gabe in and then showed him to "our best room for the Senator."

The implied privilege of power bothered Gabe. He never flaunted his position in the Senate and regretted that he had asked his aide to research accommodations and make this reservation. The connection with the innkeeper became more official as a result. Gabe hoped that he never embraced the expectation that he should receive special consideration as a member of the country's power elite, even though he now realized into his first term in the Senate how much power he and the other ninety-nine representatives wielded. He served on the Committee on Energy and Resources where major environmental decisions were made that affected every American, not just the Virginians who had elected him.

He remained firmly resolved to use any power granted him by virtue of his office accomplishing only good things that benefited his constituents.

Gabe tossed his duffel bag onto the upholstered

bench at the foot of the intricately carved wood, four poster bed. He sat down on the edge of the king-sized mattress and gazed around the suite imagining that Skye, the innkeepers' daughter, would love this place with the ambience of a vintage home yet all the amenities of a modern hotel.

Sharon flitted through his mind, a dramatic contrast to soft, gentle Skye. Like Skye, Sharon was beautiful and sexually magnetic. The similarities ended there. He had suspected from the first time Sharon had sidled up to him exuding seduction after his thoroughbred had won the Kentucky Derby that his former fiancée's ambitions centered around Gabe's old money pedigree. She would have skipped several rungs climbing the millionaire ladder simply by marrying him. Her possible designs on his money hadn't mattered much to him since he had no problem with the prospect of sharing his family inheritances and his stake in the farm's champion thoroughbreds with his wife. But when he committed to the ideal of public service and confided his intention to donate his entire senatorial salary to nonprofits working to end hunger in the U.S., Sharon apparently had balked at the prospect and promptly looked elsewhere for marriage material.

He had much to learn about Skye's nature, but he already knew that his power job didn't matter to her, and he suspected that his bank account mattered even less. He thumbed the home button on his phone to check the time and then checked the walking distance to Marin Art Gallery. He had enough time for a quick shower and change of clothes before leaving for the after-hours private showing he had personally arranged last evening.

****

At eight p.m., Gabe pressed the button to the right of the doorjamb and peered through the plate glass. The bell chime echoed from inside the gallery. Moments later the interior lights flashed on and a slim brunette clad in blue jeans and a starched white blouse came into view. She ducked behind an ebony lacquered, cube-shaped desk positioned on the far-left side of the room. Her right hand lowered beneath the edge of the desk, and a loud buzzer sounded. Gabe responded to the signal, pushing open the door as the lock disengaged with a loud click.

The young woman skirted the desk, patted the bun at the back of her neck, and then stood with her arms at her sides as Gabe approached her.

He extended his right hand. "Miss Alvaro?"

"That's right." She shook Gabe's hand. "A pleasure to meet you, Senator Hartley. I'm sorry that my father isn't here this evening. He had a prior commitment and asked me to send his regrets. He's disappointed that he won't meet you and personally guide you in viewing our collections."

"No problem. Thank you very much for accommodating me."

Gabe scanned the layout of the expansive, rectangular room. A ten-foot round, white leather bench was centered on the high gloss, blonde wood flooring. The ceiling and a border, one foot down from the ceiling around the snow-white walls, was painted matte black. Strip lights on the ceiling angled illumination down onto each canvas framed with thin black wood.

The owner's daughter drifted toward the bench and faced Gabe, her figure surrounded by downlit paintings.

"We have varied themes in our collections. Are you interested in any subject or style? Perhaps, I might recommend pieces for your office…or your home?"

"Actually, I'm interested in a specific artist. Skye Layton."

She clasped her hands together, her brown eyes sparkling. "Your timing is impeccable. I just displayed ten of her pieces after we closed at five today. She'll be here tomorrow evening for a private exhibition and reception. We're delighted she's willing to make a personal appearance. You're most welcome to attend, Senator. My father would be thrilled."

She ushered him forward toward the back of the gallery and waved her hand at the wall in front of them. "Here are the ten pieces in this store. If you don't see anything of interest here and you're still in the area two days from now, Skye has another showing in our sister shop up the coast, Angeles Art Gallery. Enjoy. Skye Layton is a luminary in our world."

She's pretty luminous in my world, too. "I'm sure I'll find something I like now." He drifted to the far-left corner and halted in front of a four by three-foot painting.

Miss Alvaro withdrew leaving him to drink in Skye's talent at his own pace.

He expelled an appreciative breath gazing at her first painting: a simple landscape of churning sea meeting cloudy sky that seemed impossibly tangible, as if he could taste the salt spray on his lips, feel the undertow of the wave suck at his feet, and experience smallness beneath the majestic dome of sky. Gabe loved the exhilarating rush he experienced watching the waves from the beach, and Skye's painting was the next best thing to being there.

He moved on to the next piece: a trio of men fishing off a splintered wood pier, three coolers at their feet. Their salt spiked hair and the craggy lines on their tanned faces spoke to days lived outdoors near the sea. One man clenched a pipe between his lips. Gabe could almost smell the thin smoke vapor seemingly whipped toward him by the ocean winds over the pier.

His admiration for Skye's talent increased viewing each consecutive painting: a lone sad-faced pelican poised to lift off a salt encrusted pylon; ethereal white ibises in flight, like nature's angels; three reddish dolphins surfing a wave, seemingly winking at him; a huge, pearlescent seashell, its intricate striations attesting to God's artistic talent.

The next work transfixed Gabe. The mermaid in profile floated in an oceanic aquarium, the scales of her tail iridescent silver, mirror-like. Her slim arm artfully crossed over her chest concealing the curve of her breasts, and her long coppery hair haloed her head partially obscuring her face. But the pale-skinned plane of her forehead, nose, and cheek struck him as intimately familiar. He had to own that painting, and Gabe felt fortunate that he had avoided any competition from would-be buyers granted this private showing.

"Do you have any questions?"

Gabe glanced back at Miss Alvaro. "One right now. Do you do the framing here?"

She sauntered over to him. "We can. Skye shipped the collection to us framed as you see here. We can easily remove the wood strips and reframe with museum quality frames in various price ranges. Would you like me to show you the catalog?"

"I would, yes."

"Certainly."

She bustled over to the desk, and he turned away from Skye's collection to join her.

Bowing his head over the open catalog he pointed to a rose gold, burnished frame. "This one. For the painting of the mermaid, please."

"Excellent. Would you like your purchase shipped?"

"I'd like to finish viewing the rest of the exhibit."

"Of course. I'll write up the paperwork for that painting and the frame. Take all the time you need."

He paced to the corner of the gallery and worked his way back to the mermaid, although he didn't need to look further having already made up his mind.

Gabe strode back to the desk.

She handed him a clipboard. "If you please, complete the shipping and contact information. Would you prefer an invoice, or will you use a credit card for the painting and frame?"

"I'll charge everything. I want the entire collection. But only reframe the mermaid, please."

Her eyebrows shot up. "Uh…" she croaked. "All *ten*?"

He grinned. "Yes. Don't go into shock on me now."

"Sir. You haven't even asked a single price."

"Oh right. I guess I should." He slipped his wallet out of his back pocket and fished out a black credit card.

Gabe handed her the card. "How much do I owe you?"

"I, uh, I… Please give me a minute. I'd like to

place a quick call to my father."

"Sure."

She started to move away and then halted turning back towards him. "Can I uh, get you anything while you wait? A glass of champagne…"

He shook his head. "No, I'm good."

She scurried away. After he filled out his address information for his Georgetown and Virginia residences and placed the clipboard down on the desk, he returned to stare at the mermaid painting as if answering a siren's call.

Miss Alvaro quickly returned, now seemingly composed and in charge. "My father is pleased to provide you with a discount and assures you that it will not affect the artist's commissions—only the gallery's profit on the showing." She handed him a slip of paper. "This represents a ten percent overall discount."

Gabe read the price and gave her a nod in approval. "Much less than I supposed. I view this as a savvy investment."

"Let me just complete all the paperwork. I should probably contact Skye Layton to inform her. Hmm…" She rubbed her hand over her chin. "She might want to cancel the reception."

"I'd prefer you keep my purchase of the collection confidential. Of course, the artist can decide about her reception. If she chooses to proceed, leave the exhibit mounted so that she can show her work. Afterward, please ship to me."

He pointed to the front of the gallery. "I wrote down two shipping addresses on the paperwork on your desk. Please ship the mermaid to my Georgetown address after reframing. The rest should go to my address in Virginia."

"Certainly. I'll just be a moment and then I'll need your signature."

While he waited Gabe browsed Skye's exhibit again. The last painting in the row drew his focus. The perspective narrowed into the far distance along a wave fringed beach on a silhouette of a boy. In the right foreground, sea oats waved against the salt bleached planks of a building. The waves, sand, sky, seagrass, and wood planks were varying shades of gray and charcoal—the silhouette black. Three crimson butterflies circled the boy's head adding triple splashes of eye-popping color.

Chapter 8

Skye's body clock stubbornly remained on east coast time, so she began her jog along the La Jolla Cove beach forty-five minutes before her cell phone's prediction of sunrise. Halting sporadically, she added twenty or more photos to her digital library as the California sky was streaked with vibrant shades of pink, purple and tangerine at dawn. The wealth of glorious vistas she had stored in her photo library made her eager to return to her studio to start painting.

After a luxurious, hot shower she dressed in shorts and a T-shirt and then tiptoed into the empty kitchen. She filled an oversized mug with boiling water from the sink spigot, plopped in a tea bag to steep, and strolled over to the floor to ceiling windows. Beyond the glass panes, tranquil waves reflected brilliant sun sparkles.

She turned at the sound of the front door opening. Karol's four dogs raced into the room, each plopping down and rolling over at Skye's feet begging for belly rubs. Happy to oblige, she raised her head as footsteps advanced toward her.

"Good morning," John Paul said.

The sound of his voice prompted the foursome to wiggle upright and scamper over to him repeating the roll and belly rub begging at his feet.

"Morning," Skye said. "They love you."

"Only because they know after their walk, they get treats." All four dogs sprang up and stampeded into the kitchen.

"And they know exactly where the treats are." He chuckled softly. "Do you need anything?"

"No, thanks." She gave a nod toward the kitchen counter. "That tea is perfect."

Skye walked into the kitchen with him and picked up the mug.

"I'll be right with you," he said.

Back in the great room, Skye sank down onto the couch and leaned her head on the soft cushion behind her.

John Paul came over to the seating area toting a mug of coffee and sat down next to her. "So, tonight is your big night."

She shrugged her shoulders. "I guess so."

He knit his brows. "You don't sound excited. Don't you want to do the show?"

"Well, yes...but not really. I'm not used to all the attention, standing around listening to people critique your work hoping someone will appreciate a piece enough to buy it. Very nerve wracking to say the least."

She prickled under his piercing gaze. "Enough about me. What do you do, besides providing excellent help to my aunt and her pups?"

His sober expression confused her.

"Right now, I work for my dad a bit and I'm a personal trainer, plus, I guess, a butler of sorts here." His flat tone was unmistakable.

"You're not happy," she concluded.

He sighed. "I'm sorry that I gave you that impression—especially about working for Karol. Actually, sometimes memories...well..."

John Paul heaved a breath. "I was about to leave

for freshman year at college when my mom was diagnosed with cancer. I had to regroup. I wanted to spend what little time she had left with her every day. She passed quickly."

"I'm so sorry, John Paul."

"Thank you," he said. "It was rough, and it kind of paralyzed me for a while. I didn't know what to do with my life. Thank God, my dad was understanding and supportive. I did eventually go to college, but my heart wasn't in it. I quit after a semester and bummed around for a while living back home and helping my dad with his business, and then I met Karol. She asked me if I would dog sit for her here at her house. She was leaving on a two-week trip to Greece, and she hated to board them. I've always loved dogs, and I jumped at the chance to get away for a while. Long story short; that was four years ago, and I wound up moving in here at her invitation. I never went back to live with Dad. I still help him out at work, and the gym I started going to years ago hired me as a trainer. My life now is good, and I owe it all to your aunt."

"Aunt Karol is a very special woman."

"Yes, she is. Now I better move. I have to feed the girls before I go to the gym. Can I fix your breakfast before I leave? An omelet? Toast?"

"No, thank you. I'm good."

"Have a nice day. I'll see you tonight at the gallery."

"You're coming to my show?"

"Of course. I wouldn't miss it. It's all your aunt has talked about for weeks. See you later."

Skye finished her tea and then ambled into the kitchen to rinse the mug. From somewhere overhead a chorus of barks sounded. She climbed the stairs following the noise. The dogs lined up on their haunches in the threshold of the open doorway to her aunt's studio.

"All right, ladies, you may come in," came Aunt Karol's lilting voice.

The dogs disappeared through the doorway in a split second as Skye approached the studio. She peeked inside. Her aunt sat cross-legged on the hard wood floor lavishing the pups with her attention. Skye gazed around the room which reminded Skye of her beloved workroom on the top floor of the Inn of the Three Butterflies. The walls of the studio, like hers, were painted a buttery yellow. Sunshine streamed through three banks of windows like the lighting at home that she so prized. An easel stood in front of the largest window facing the Pacific. No blinds or window dressings obscured the ocean and sky panorama.

The canvas on the easel magnetized Skye: a raging storm over a furious, roiling sea. If Skye didn't know her aunt's capability for realism with her brushwork, she'd swear that the image was a blow up of a photo.

Skye entered the studio. "I can hear the thunder and feel the rain sting my face. Amazing work."

"Thank you, honey." Karol stood and wiped her hands on a towel she had tucked into the waist band of her jeans. "I have a few more touches to add and then, done. I heard you leave the house early this morning."

"Oh. I'm so sorry if I woke you."

"You didn't. I was already here in the studio. I couldn't sleep. I'm sure you know how it feels when a painting calls you."

"I definitely do. My easel is fairly screaming at me

to paint the myriad of photos I've taken during my trip. I didn't expect the beauty of the mountains ringing the Coachella Valley to grab my imagination the way they have."

"I'm sure Antonio will want a chance to show any new paintings of California." She waved a hand toward the easel. "This piece is earmarked for the La Jolla gallery."

"Who is Antonio?"

"He owns the Marin gallery where your show is tonight and also the gallery in Newport Beach hosting your next show." Karol glanced at her watch. "We have an appointment with him this morning to make sure you're happy with how he displayed your paintings. Then, I thought we could hit the stores and find something lovely for you to wear to the show and to dinner tonight." She wrapped her arm around Skye's shoulder. "Let's change clothes. Sound good?"

Skye nodded.

****

Skye relaxed in the passenger seat of Karol's car enjoying the view during the drive along the coastline. "I was surprised when John Paul told me he's going to the show tonight."

"He probably helped hang some of your paintings."

"I don't understand. Why would John Paul hang my paintings?"

"Oh, darling, didn't I tell you? John Paul is Antonio's son. He and his sister work part time at the gallery."

"I see. Well, that makes sense now. He did mention that he helps his father and is an athletic trainer. Busy guy."

The gallery was located across the street from the Coast Boulevard Park. Palm trees swayed in the light breeze. Runners, walkers, some with dogs on leashes, milled along the path fronting the ocean. Karol parked the car behind the gallery. They hopped out of the car, traversed an alleyway between two buildings, and rounded the front corner of the gallery, stopping in front of the glass door. Karol's finger hovered over the doorbell. A buzzer sounded before she pushed the button.

"Bella, you're finally here. Late as usual." A tall, muscular, striking gentleman with salt and pepper hair, clad in a perfectly tailored charcoal gray suit, powder blue dress shirt, and cobalt blue silk tie embraced Karol—with seemingly full body contact.

His crystal blue eyes held Skye's gaze over Karol's shoulder. "And you must be the gifted Skye Layton. The family resemblance is undeniable."

He partially released Karol draping one arm over her shoulder and extended a large, tanned hand toward Skye. She placed her hand in his.

"It's a pleasure to finally meet you, Miss Layton. I'm Antonio Alvaro, and I'm humbled that you chose my gallery to represent your work."

"The pleasure is mine." She shook his hand and then surveyed the brightly lit space. "You have a lovely gallery, Mr. Alvaro."

"Please, my friends call me Antonio, and I hope you will think of me as your friend." He casually massaged her aunt's shoulder. The warm expression on her aunt's face at the man's attention spoke volumes.

"Look around as long as you like. Would you ladies like something to drink? Champagne? Wine?"

"No thank you," Skye and Karol each responded.

Karol strode across the room to the far corner of the gallery halting before the painting of a pelican. "Oh my, I love this, Skye. I feel like I'm back at the inn with my sisters watching the pelicans dive for fish."

Skye strolled over to her side.

"Darn, there's a sold sticker on it," Karol groused. "I would have snapped this one right up this very minute."

"Aunt Karol." Skye gave her a warm hug. "As if I would ever let you buy one of my paintings. If I knew you wanted another pelican, I'd have sent you one immediately." Skye made a mental note to do just that as soon as she got home to thank her for the wonderful visit.

"You're out of luck today if you want to buy *any* Skye Layton painting," Antonio said. "Notice that all the paintings have sold stickers on them. The entire collection was purchased last evening after we mounted the display."

Skye gaped at him open-mouthed.

Karol widened her eyes and then threw her arms around Skye. "Every painting? Skye, that is amazing."

"It's also a first for our gallery." He beamed at Skye. "Karol's last show sold out early that night, but we have *never* had a sell out before it even opened."

"Does that mean the show is cancelled?" Skye said.

"It's too late to cancel. We have press coming, and all the invitations have gone out. We're expecting over one hundred people." Antonio walked over to the ebony desk, opened a drawer, and lifted out a bunch of pamphlets.

"My daughter, Leticia, had what I think is a

wonderful idea." He handed Skye and Karol a pamphlet which depicted photos of Skye Layton originals.

"These are the paintings for your next show at our other gallery. Leticia thought we should give the pamphlets to our guests tonight so that they can pre-purchase them or even opt to attend that show, too...if it doesn't sell out like this one. If it does sell out tonight, we have time to cancel the show in Newport Beach. What do you think?"

Karol floated over to Antonio. "I think Leticia is a genius." She necklaced her arms around his neck gazing up at him—adoringly.

"Hmm," Skye said drawing her aunt's attention.

Karol turned her head toward Skye. "You might sell out another show tonight! Antonio, now we *need* champagne." She clapped her hands together gleefully.

Antonio strode away.

"I can't believe this is happening." Skye sank down onto the desk chair. "I hoped that I'd sell at least one painting. I never dreamed I'd sell them all the first time I showed here."

"Oh, honey. You've always underestimated your talent. Antonio is my friend and..."

"*Just* your friend?"

"Well..." Her face lit with a broad grin. "That's a conversation for another time. What I was going to say was, Antonio *is* my friend, but he's a superb businessman. He would never agree to show an artist's work if he didn't think the talent was worth promoting. And he hasn't made an exception for you."

Antonio returned carrying a silver tray holding three flutes and a bottle of champagne in an ice bucket. After filling the glasses, he distributed them and then raised his flute. "To your first successful show at Marin gallery. I hope you'll allow me many more in the future."

Skye took a delicious sip utterly delighted at this unexpected success.

"And one more toast." Antonio said. "I would also like to toast the patron who bought all your paintings."

Skye almost choked on her drink. "Wait a minute. *What?* Are you saying one person bought everything?"

"Yes. I am. Another first for Marin Gallery." He topped off his and Karol's glasses.

"Who is he? Or…she?" Skye's hand trembled. She set her glass down on the desktop.

"I'm sorry. I'm not at liberty to say."

Skye stared at him in disbelief.

"You must, Antonio," Karol insisted.

"Bella, you know I can't. All transactions are private except for business to business. I wasn't here when the customer came in. Leticia handled the sale."

"I would love to invite this person to my dinner tonight after the show. Please, Antonio." Karol trained imploring eyes on him.

"I can't give you the number."

Karol's sweet expression darkened into a frown.

"But. I will make a phone call and extend the invitation for you. It's the best I can do."

Karol narrowed her eyes to slits but gave Antonio a half smile.

She grinned at Skye placing her flute on the silver tray. "I guess we'll have to wait until tonight to meet your mystery patron."

Skye stood and hugged Antonio. "Thank you for everything."

"Absolutely my pleasure."

"Let's go shopping. I think we both need a drop-dead gorgeous dress for the dinner party." Karol bussed a kiss on Antonio's cheek and led Skye out the door.

Chapter 9

"You look divine!" Karol balled her hands on her hips and beamed as she appraised Skye's outfit.

"Really?" Skye lowered her gaze to the sparkly, strapless, emerald sequined cocktail dress and glittery, crystal encrusted high heels that she wore.

"Yes. Absolutely. I knew those shoes would show off your legs. There are a few eligible bachelors on my guest list. You'll take their breath away."

Skye waved off her aunt's compliments. The only eligible bachelor she'd like to rob of breath was Gabriel. She wondered where he was, and if she might dominate his thoughts as he did hers.

"Thanks. But look at you," Skye said.

Karol wore an Armani snow white pants suit that fit her so perfectly it seemed sewn to her slim body. Her russet hair, nearly as long as Skye's, was wound into a chignon at the nape of her neck. "You look stunning."

Suddenly a wave of homesickness swept over Skye. Her aunt looked so much like her mom. She wished that Kay was there with her to celebrate this unbelievable success. How Skye would appreciate having her lively hostess mom at her elbow all evening to handle the expected small talk with Karol's guests. She consoled herself delighting in the knowledge that she could return home the next day with no need to stay for another show. Those pieces earmarked for her second gallery show had sold out at the Marin gallery earlier that evening.

The doorbell chimed an echoing pealing in the high-ceilinged vestibule of the mansion.

"Showtime." Karol hung her arm over Skye's shoulders and led her out of the guest room down the upstairs hallway.

Skye pulled up short at the top of the stairs gaping down at Gabriel Hartley conversing with John Paul in the open doorway. Just a glimpse of his profile sparked elation as if he lit a match to an explosion of joy inside her. Trembling, she nudged Aunt Karol back into the hall away from the landing.

"What's wrong?" Karol sputtered.

"How do you know Gabriel Hartley, Aunt Karol?"

"Who?"

"Senator Gabriel Hartley from Virginia."

"Now that you mention it, I do think I've heard of him. But I don't know him."

Skye frowned. "Then you didn't invite him here?"

Karol wagged her head. "I'm so confused. Do you know him?"

"Yes."

"Ah…your young man. With the turbulence."

"That's him. And he's downstairs talking with John Paul. I wonder why?"

Karol linked her elbow through Skye's. "Let's go ask him why he's crashing my party."

Equally thrilled and shocked at his magical appearance here, Skye let her aunt tow her to the head of the staircase. Gabriel still lingered in the foyer. He raised his head and locked eyes with Skye as she gazed down at him. His brown eyes danced. "Hello, Skye."

Just the sound of his resonant voice triggered rills

of pleasure through her. "Hi, Gabriel." Skye floated down the stairs toward him, her right hand lightly grazing the banister on her descent.

Only slightly aware of Karol behind her, Skye placed her hand on his outstretched palm. He wrapped his fingers around her hand and drew her close enough for her to drink in his clean, woodsy scent and feel the emanating warmth near him. "How?" she simply said.

"I received an invitation to dinner this afternoon through Antonio Alvaro." He gave her a mischievous grin, his dark chocolate eyes twinkling.

It took Skye several seconds to make the connection. She threw back her head and belly laughed. "You!"

Karol touched Skye's shoulder. "Will you introduce us, Skye?"

Grinning from ear to ear, Skye said, "Karol Binder O'Rourke, this is Senator Gabriel Hartley. Gabriel, my aunt Karol."

Gabriel released Skye's hand long enough to shake Karol's hand and then casually linked hands again with Skye. "It's a pleasure to meet you, Miz Binder O'Rourke. I'm a great fan of your art."

"Karol, please, Senator. I'm flattered that you're familiar with my work."

"Please call me Gabe. I have several pieces, both inherited and purchased. We've actually met before, although it was a long time ago. I attended one of your showings in Virginia Beach with my father when I was a kid."

Karol widened her eyes. "My goodness. That had to be, what, twenty-five years ago? It was probably one of my first shows. Skye has taken after me in that regard. She started showing her art at the same gallery."

"Twenty-five years ago sounds about right. Dad wanted to add a little culture to my life. He was an avid collector. I learned to love art through him."

"Aunt Karol, I'm pretty sure that Gabriel is here because he was the mystery patron who bought out my show at Marin Gallery."

Karol's eyebrows shot up.

"Yes, that's true." Gabriel's cheeks dimpled with his roguish grin. "How could I not?"

"You have excellent taste," Karol said.

He gazed pointedly at Skye.

Aunt Karol winked at her. "In many things." She patted the side of Gabriel's arm and then kissed Skye's cheek softly. "I need to do a little rearranging of place cards for dinner."

The doorbell sounded, a three-note bong that registered as an alarming gong to Skye. She gave a start leaning into Gabriel's chest. He embraced her lightly, whispering in her hair, "I missed you."

Magic. His effect on her banished her anxiety and warmed every cold, lonely part of her. Could she possibly find in him all the romance and love she had missed harboring her secrets? For now, she hoped, yes.

Skye gazed up into his gleaming eyes. "I missed you, too. Would you like to go outside for a drink?"

"If you would."

A breeze lifted wisps of Skye's hair that framed her face as John Paul opened the door and ushered two guests inside into the hallway.

"Senator Hartley?" A woman wearing a flowing maxiskirt, peasant blouse, and wrist to elbow bangle bracelets scurried over to Gabriel and Skye.

"Yes, ma'am," he said, his expression sober—pleasant, cool, so different than the devilish, smoldering smile that had bloomed on his face looking up at Skye moments ago.

"What brings you to California? Are the rumors true that you might run for President? I'd vote for you in a minute."

He shook his head. "Thank you for your vote of confidence. But that's the farthest thing from my mind." Gabriel chuckled. "And probably the Republican party's, too. I'm actually in California for showings of Skye Layton's work."

"Ah," she said nodding. She glanced at Skye. "Then, please take my business card. I won't leave here tonight until I have a chance to invite Ms. Layton to show in my gallery in Tucson. You might want to visit my gallery, Senator, if she accepts."

"I'd be delighted, thank you." Gabriel pocketed the card. "Please excuse us."

He steered Skye toward the patio doors. Her heart beat faster just having him at her side, and she looked forward to, instead of dreading, the evening ahead.

"Are you really going to run for President?" Skye wasn't sure how she'd react if he said, yes.

"Never say never, but no." He trained soft eyes on her face. "I'm not sure I'll even run for reelection to the Senate next term. Navigating the power corridors in Washington is tricky. I'm determined to maintain my moral compass. Maybe that's not possible long term in D.C."

His intentions struck Skye as pure and admirable. And rare in a politician. Not that she had any experience judging one politician from another. She only knew that she was powerfully attracted to him. Skye was more than ready to believe that he meant what he said.

Outside, the balmy air felt silken on Skye's bare arms and shoulders. The scents of bonfires and barbecues floated on the breeze. Fairy lights lined the folds of the white tent's ceiling that housed a long dinner table set for twenty. With Gabriel's happy appearance here, her earlier jitters had disappeared. His open affection buoyed her confidence and made her feel less unworthy to be the guest of honor at a fancy dinner. She still missed walking barefoot on her beach on the Outer Banks, but there, in that moment, she only wanted to be with him.

Gabriel left her standing at the opening of the tent while he went to the bar for champagne. Relaxed and peaceful, Skye greeted several guests as they came into the tent to take their places at the table. When he returned, he handed her a flute and lifted his. "A toast to the resounding success of your debut in the West Coast art scene."

She clinked her glass against his and took a lovely, heady sip. "About that. Since you were the sole buyer at Marin Gallery, I'm way less impressed about my pre-showing sell out. Was this some sort of a grand gesture? Um…" Skye hesitated to admit a suspicion that had suddenly taken hold. "Are there strings attached?"

"What? Why would there be strings to my buying beautiful art?"

Arching her eyebrows, she angled her head and gazed at him pointedly.

He huffed a laugh. "Oh, I see. Maybe you'd feel

somehow beholden to me. Owe me a return favor of something. Is that what you're thinking?"

Skye twisted her lips. "Something like that."

"Absolutely, no." He tipped a finger under her chin. His penetrating gaze transfixed Skye and transmitted clearly that she needed to truly hear the next thing he'd say. "I admired your work the second I viewed the collection and snapped up the chance to make a savvy investment. But as much as I appreciate the art, that cannot compare to how I feel about the artist."

A jolt of pleasure stunned her. The man literally took her breath away. "Thank you, Gabriel, truly. On both counts: professional and personal."

"You're more than welcome."

He crooked his elbow. "Shall we?"

Smiling up at him she hooked a hand over his firm bicep and sighed as he tucked it close to his heart.

"Let's go make these gallery owners' night. I hope you can keep up with demand."

Skye snorted a laugh. "It would be a great problem to have."

****

Every minute he had spent with her intrigued Gabe more. Skye presented a rare challenge to a man used to the advances of aggressive women with high aspirations. He rarely had to win a female over, quite the opposite. If anything, his power and wealth were probably disadvantages in pursuing Skye, a total reversal. Pursuing a woman at all was a total reversal for Gabe. And he had every intention of pursuing this gentle, unassuming beauty.

He liked that she didn't hog the dinner

conversation, even though who she was and what she had to say were essentially what the dinner was about in the first place. Instead, she deflected praise and compliments, answered any questions sweetly and briefly and asked insightful, personal questions about the patrons' and gallery owners' interests and businesses.

Another thing he found that he liked enormously—he didn't have to talk at all. What a refreshing relief to not occupy the center of a dinner table discussion. Gabe was so used to the firing line, he felt like he had received a stay of execution for the night.

Powerful emotions had grown in intensity as the evening progressed. His position in the national limelight came with the job he loved more than hated, and he accepted the negatives without complaint. But how wonderful if his personal life, maybe his home life, might be a haven of peace.

Sitting by her side all evening, inhaling Skye's jasmine perfume, Gabe had felt peaceful believing that the serendipity of meeting her pointed him clearly toward his future.

Gabe waited for all the guests to leave the mansion before he drew Skye into his arms for a good night kiss that he hoped would linger in her memory until they could see each other again.

"Mm." Her shining jade eyes sparkled with reflected moonlight and candle glow.

"What was that for?"

"It was for until…"

"Yes. Until we see each other again. I'd like that very much. When do you leave California?"

"Tonight. Whenever I can get to the jet."

"Wow. Private jet?"

"Yes, ma'am."

"Remind me to hitch a ride with you sometime." On a laugh, she arched her back which fused her lower body closer to his sending a sensual jolt straight to his brain.

Intuiting that she'd recoil at overt sexuality this soon in their relationship, he kept his libido in check. Gabe couldn't resist cupping her face with his hands and kissing her softly once more. "You're welcome to hitch a ride with me anytime. Want to come with me tonight?"

"I can't. I really want to spend this evening with Aunt Karol. She's been so good to me. I'm leaving tomorrow."

"I understand. We'll still see each other soon?"

Her spontaneous rapid-fire, "Yes," reassured him.

"That's great. Good night, Skye."

"Good night, Gabriel. Thank you for buying my paintings. And for coming here tonight."

"My pleasure."

Chapter 10

Gabe rubbed his hand over the scratchy beard stubble on his chin in frustration. The drive had come to a near standstill along Route 95. He had meant to leave his office early, so he'd escape the Friday traffic jam out of Washington, but a fifteen-minute meeting turned into over an hour, and inevitably he encountered heavy congestion out of the Capitol.

He looked forward to spending time on the farm. *If I ever get there.*

Gabe sorely missed his beloved horses and the grace and serenity of his home during his urban stints in D.C. And he missed his mother. Since his grandfather died, he made a point of speaking with Mom daily knowing how deeply she suffered in mourning her father. He shared her sorrow and even missed the morning emails from his grandfather commenting on any news clips that he thought important for Gabe. God forbid the Senator didn't approve of the shirt or tie he spied on his grandson in a photo. Gabe laughed out loud remembering the thunder amid the sunshine that was his granddad. *Man, I miss you, Sir.*

Road weary from the normally three hours, now doubled trip, he turned off Route 13 and followed the tree-lined, meandering lane that led home. The farm's white, iron gates each topped with prominent, ornate Double MM's, signifying his grandmother's and mother's initials loomed ahead. His wife, Madelyn and daughter, Meredith were the lights of Granddad's life. Madelyn died when his mom was a little girl sadly teaching her the lesson of crushing loss that she would relive twice with the death of his dad, and now Granddad.

Eager to spend time with Mom, he lowered the window and punched in the code on the entry keypad. Waiting for the gates to slowly swing open, he left the window down inhaling the welcome scents of home: fresh mown grass, the briny tang of the Chesapeake Bay, and pungent horse manure. Gabe longed to detour to the stables, but that would wait until morning.

As soon as the gates opened enough for his sleek sedan to squeeze through, he drove straight to the main house, a glowing antebellum beacon ahead of him with its upstairs and downstairs windows fully lit. He bet Mom had waited dinner for him.

Finally released from the confines of the car, he took the front stairs two at a time and opened the never locked, heavy, mahogany door. His mother stood in the foyer just outside the arc of the swinging door. The expression on her face reminded him of her greeting him after missed curfews in his teens. Meredith Hartley was a force to be reckoned with.

"Gabriel, I'm so disappointed that you didn't keep your word. You promised me that you would leave early so we can have dinner together." She rose onto her tiptoes and pecked his cheek with a light kiss.

"Sorry, a meeting ran over and then the traffic…"

She spun on her heel and strode briskly away from him toward the dining room. Gabe understood from her no-nonsense posture that she fully expected him to follow her.

"…was unbearable," he said to her retreating back. "And hello to you, too, Mother. Why so formal tonight?" Gabe took in the glittering tapers in shiny silver candlesticks on the claw-footed, mahogany table with seating for fourteen, and the matching sideboard laden with food in the elegant dining room. Platters of carved turkey, roast beef, and sliced cheeses; a basket of pretzel rolls; and bowls heaped with a variety of salads piqued his appetite.

Meredith, who was impeccably dressed in a peach, linen pantsuit wearing her prized pearl necklace, perched on her seat at the head of the table gazing at him evenly.

Gabe pulled out a heavy chair and sat down on the silk upholstered seat. "Why aren't we eating in the kitchen?"

"You haven't been home in a while. I wanted to make this evening special." She snapped her napkin unfolded and spread it over her lap. "I have all your favorites."

Which happen to be all Grandad's favorites, too. Gabe stretched out his arm over the tabletop and clasped her small-boned, fragile hand.

He frowned. "You look tired and way too thin, Mother. Are you sleeping well and eating all your meals?"

"Don't be tedious." She waved a hand dismissively.

Meredith gave a nod toward the sideboard. "I'll have some of that pasta salad, please."

Gabe shoved back from the table, his and her dinner plates in hand. He scooped out two large helpings for each of them and returned to his seat.

"I haven't had this salad in so long," he said after indulging in a mouthful of pepperoni laced pasta—his hands-down favorite. "Thanks for making this for me."

"You are most welcome." She nibbled at her food.

Gabe rose again and fixed a roast beef sandwich and a second sandwich of ham and Swiss cheese. He rapidly wolfed down the meal.

Sated, he wiped his mouth with a napkin and leaned back in his chair. "That really hit the spot. Thanks."

"I'm glad you liked it. You'll have to take the leftovers back with you." She sipped a glass of wine beaming at him.

"I never turn down food, especially your pepperoni pasta salad."

"It's so good to have you home. The delivery you told me to expect came today. I had Bradley uncrate the paintings. He put them in the living room."

Bradley Thompson, his grandfather's righthand man on the horse farm, remained dedicated to his mom's family. Gabe appreciated Bradley's staying on after his grandfather's death. Knowing that Bradley lived in one of the houses on the property comforted Gabe and assured him that a trusted friend looked after his mother in his frequent absences.

"I'm impressed with your taste. You certainly have your grandfather's eye for art. He would have loved the paintings of the dolphins and pelicans."

"I thought of him when I browsed in the gallery. I might hang one or two of them in the beach cottage. Take whatever you want for the main house. I'll put the rest in my house here until I decide where they belong."

"Thank you. There's one that caught my eye. I

swear it looks just like your grandfather's cottage..." She cleared her throat. "I should say your cottage." Her voice quivered.

"Uh…"

Gabe's spirits sank in empathy. His mother's speech never faltered.

She took a deep breath and then continued, "The little boy reminds me so much of you climbing the dunes."

"You know, it might just be grandfather's cottage in the painting," Gabe mused. "The artist lives on the Outer Banks. I'll bet she's seen it. She really captures the magic of the sandbar.

"I was struck by the almost photographic realism in her paintings. Such enormous talent. I purchased every piece from her planned showing the night before, after hours at the gallery," Gabe said.

She tilted her head and narrowed her eyes.

"What?" he said reacting to her quizzical expression.

"Her paintings are simply signed Skye. Who is this?"

"Her name is Skye Layton. Perhaps that sounds familiar? She apparently has already made quite a name for herself."

"And how did you find this new artist?"

"We met at Mark's wedding. She's Lynn's best friend and was her Maid of Honor. Almost everyone talked about her talent. I had to go the gallery to see what the buzz was all about. I was blown away. You know her Aunt Karol's work."

"Really? The name, Karol as an artist doesn't ring a bell, either. What is her last name?"

"Does O'Rourke ring a bell?

She gasped. "K.B. O'Rourke? She did the painting your dad gave me for our tenth anniversary."

"I know."

Gabe had heard the story many times. His parents had honeymooned in Greece. They had fallen in love with a tiny restaurant on their first night on the island of Milos and had never gone to another restaurant the entire week. A little over nine years later, Dad had seen a painting of that very restaurant in an art magazine and had to purchase it for his wife. Gabe had neglected to mention the painting to Karol when they had met. He made a mental note to ask her about it when he saw her next having often wondered what lengths his father had to go to surprise his mother.

"When I look at that painting, I can hear the waves and smell the ocean and the food cooking. It brings me right back to that magical week every time," she said.

"I'll tell her how much you treasure the painting the next time I see her."

"Next time? You talked to her? Was she at Mark's wedding, too?"

"No, she wasn't. Karol hosted a dinner after the art showing for Skye Layton. Karol is an interesting woman. You'll love her when you meet her."

"And I would meet her…why?"

Gabe paused introspective, contemplating his certainty that Skye's family and his would meet. Maybe merge. "I bet she'll show her work on the East Coast again. We'll go together if she does."

"I'd love that." She rose from the table and started to clear the dishes.

Gabe caught his mother's hand. "You look

exhausted. I'll take care of clean up. Get some sleep."

"Nonsense. Your work and long drive were much more exhausting than my day. I have this under control. Go settle in."

He helped carry the plates and platters into the kitchen anyway before he headed to his car to drive the few minutes to his house.

His grandfather had hired the builders of the ranch style, white cottage when Gabe had turned eighteen so that he would have his own space on the farm and could, in his grandad's words, "sow some wild oats without his mother knowing what time he got home."

Inside the house, Gabe switched on the lights in the small living room, grabbed the remote off the coffee table, and powered up the flat-screen TV that spanned one entire wall. With the news channel droning background noise, he walked down the hallway into the bedroom, stripped off his clothes, and turned on the shower nozzles to just short of scalding. When he finished, he dried with a towel around his waist giving half an ear to the news broadcast. Apparently, nothing newsworthy had occurred since the last time Gabe had tuned in, so he ambled into the living room, turned off the TV and lights, reversed to his room, and climbed into bed naked.

He propped his back against a pillow leaning on the headboard and scrolled through unread emails on his phone. Nothing needed his immediate attention. He closed the mail app, noted the time, and decided to call the woman who'd been on his mind all day.

****

Skye lifted her brush from the canvas, stepped back from the easel, and assessed her work. The eyes of the birds she had painted seemed to follow her movement. Yep, she thought. *Just what I was going for.*

She stepped forward to touch up one of the black masks on the waxwing in the foreground and then placed the brush into a cup of the Mona Lisa solvent she preferred. Arching her back, she held the stretch with her palms flat against her spine. Her curtains billowed in the light breeze through the window screen. Skye inhaled deeply the fresh, honeysuckle scented air, happy to be home despite how much she had enjoyed the trip West. Her creative juices had flowed freely since returning from California, and her studio was lined with paintings.

One large painting caught her critical eye. She was pleased overall with her rendering of the stunning mountains encircling Palm Springs. Gazing at those mountains, the party at the clubhouse where she had met Gabriel blazed in her memory. The scene was so vivid that she imagined she felt his lips on hers, equal parts shock and quickfire attraction.

Her cell phone buzzed on the coffee table distracting her from the wonderful memory.

She answered the call without first checking the caller ID readout, assuming it was one of her sisters. "What time are you leaving in the morning? I can't wait to see you."

"I'll be on the next plane. I'll be there first thing in the morning." Gabriel's now familiar voice instead of Bree's or Summer's quickened Skye's pulse.

"Oh! Hi. I thought you were someone else."

"Well now I'm jealous."

Skye huffed a laugh, suddenly school-girl giddy. She paced in lazy circles around her studio. "No reason to be. I thought you were one of my sisters. They're both coming tomorrow to help open the inn for the season. It's one of my favorite times. This year will be even better. With Bree married and Summer engaged, we haven't found much time alone, just the three of us. We call it sister time. It's sacred.... I'm babbling. I'm sorry."

"Don't apologize. I called just to hear your voice."

You did? Her heart raced, and she grinned widely.

"I miss you," he said.

A burst of elation coursed through Skye. Should she tell him that she rarely stopped thinking about him? That she thought of him each night before she went to sleep, that she dreamed about him, and that he was her first waking thought every day? Should she say, I miss you, too?

He continued the casual conversation before she could decide on a response. "I'm spending this weekend at the farm. I bet your ears were ringing not too long ago."

"Really? Why?"

"My mother had all your paintings uncrated by the time I arrived this evening, and she was curious about the artist. I told her how we met..."

"Oh really? *Exactly* how we met?"

His hearty laughter boomed in her ear.

"No, nothing about the, uh, kiss attack. But I told her about the wedding, buying out your showing, and meeting your Aunt Karol at dinner. She was very impressed with your work."

"Thank you, Gabriel. I'm glad."

"You call me Gabriel. Except for my mother, no one does. All my friends call me Gabe, and you are certainly much more than a friend to me. My mother usually refers to me as Gabriel when she's disappointed in me." He chuckled. "Which is most of the time."

"Gabriel is such a lyrical name, but okay, I'll call you Gabe from now on. I don't want you to think I'm disappointed in you."

"Good."

With her phone pressed to her ear, she drifted over to her window and gazed at the pale-yellow ribbon of moonlight riding the waves. His silence persisted.

She shut the window preparing to close her studio for the night. "Well…goodnight, Gabe. Thank you for calling."

"Wait," he said. "Before you go, I'm trying to envision you. Where are you? What are you wearing?"

He belted out a laugh apparently amused at his presumption.

"Seriously?"

"Why not?"

"Um. Take a guess."

"Hmm. I'm picturing black lace, no wait white, definitely white lace; a short lace nightgown skimming your knees. Your hair is loose curling down your back."

"That's uncanny. Do you have a hidden camera in my studio?" Skye gazed at her reflection in the window. Her hair was piled on top of her head in a messy bun. Her sister's ancient Harvard sweatshirt fell off one shoulder, and her sweatpants hung loosely at her hips.

"What can I say? It's a gift. Now it's your turn."

No matter how hard Skye focused the vision didn't come. She could "see" her sisters, their sweethearts, her parents, and her aunts at will, but nothing came when she tried to see him. However, sensations swirled within her. She felt the pressure of his lips against hers and the electric warmth of his hand on the small of her back when he had led her to the dance floor. But she still couldn't picture him in her mind.

Skye took a stab at it anyway. "Let's see. Maybe a torn sweatshirt probably from high school and a pair of basketball shorts." Might be right. Her dad wore something similar to bed every night.

"Nailed it! Good night, pretty lady. I have a feeling I'll dream about you in white lace tonight. I'll call you soon. Have fun with your sisters."

"Good night, Gabe."

She disconnected the call. The vision of Gabe lying naked in bed atop white sheets came with stunning clarity. Skye sucked in a breath. *Oh my! I didn't nail that at all.* Switching off the lights, she headed toward her bedroom, positive about what visions would fill her dreamland that night.

Chapter 11

Skye had intended to drive to the airport to meet Summer's and Bree's synchronized arrivals from New York and Chicago so they could savor *every* minute of planned sister time. But Bonney pressed her to meet over coffee to review research about the effects of offshore oil exploration on marine life and to strategize their group's approach to impede destructive testing.

Back in her studio after the meeting with minutes to wait before her sisters' estimated arrival time, Skye thought about the looming challenges facing the coalition's mission to stop seismic testing off the shores of her home. Surely the Administration could be persuaded to understand the terrible consequences, couldn't they?

A bright vision burst in Skye's mind like the beginning of a movie. Summer wore oval sunglasses with beige and black polka dotted frames sitting at the wheel of a bronze-gold colored, mini-SUV next to Bree, who wore the exact negative of her sister's sunglasses. The car had just turned onto Oregon Inlet Road.

Skye tore out of her studio and thundered down two flights of stairs the back way into the sunny kitchen. Kay and Mike sat shoulder to shoulder on high-backed, glossy wood stools at the long beige and amber-speckled granite counter mutually peering at a laptop screen, maybe doing the inn's books.

Mike hopped off his stool and caught Skye by the shoulders with the gentle touch of his huge hands. "Whoa. Where's the fire?"

She grinned into her dad's crystal blue, twinkling eyes. "They're here."

"Well then." Mike released his hold on her immediately.

"What are we waiting for?" He held out his hand to Kay.

Mom clasped Dad's hand and eased off her stool. Skye set in motion shoving open the sliding glass door out to the deck knowing her parents would bring up the rear of the greeting party. On the run, she rounded the corner of the veranda that encircled the inn just as her sisters' rental car tires crunched over the gravel apron out front.

The driver and passenger car doors swung open, and Bree and Summer abandoned the car. Skye didn't slow down dismounting the stairs with a clatter and raced open-armed toward her sisters. The triplets slammed into a trio hug, and Skye finally felt truly whole.

She relished the circular embrace as the encompassing power of her connection with them jolted through her like sheet lightening, sorely tempting Skye to take Bree and Summer to flight to give her soaring spirit free reign. But Mom would likely kill Skye if she robbed her of an earthlier reunion with her absent girls.

On cue Kay said, "Darlings, come give me a hug."

Skye side-stepped letting her sisters loose. Bree and Summer rushed to hug Kay, and then Mike enfolded them in a hug.

The hello, so *good* to see you, missed you so much

said, they all stood in a loose circle beaming at each other.

"How about I carry your bags inside?" Mike proposed.

Summer tossed him the key fob. "Thanks, Daddy."

"You look wonderful, Bree. You wear your happiness with Jack like a halo." Kay tenderly hooked an auburn tendril of Bree's hair behind her ear. "I don't think I've ever seen you look this radiant."

"I told her the exact same thing when we met at the airport…" Summer said.

Skye surveyed her sister and certainty dawned. She locked eyes with Summer.

"I *knew* it!" Summer shouted.

Skye and Summer grabbed hold of Bree at the same time, throwing back their heads with glee as tears trailed down their cheeks.

"Why didn't you tell us?"

"How did I miss seeing this? When did you find out?"

"Wait." Kay reached out her arms cupping Bree's shoulders with her hands. "I see now! Oh, my darling!"

Kay wept openly as Bree's head bobbed yes, yes, yes. "Mike. We're going to be grandparents!"

Dad's eyes welled, and he displaced his wife and daughters drawing Bree into his arms and nearly swept her off her feet in the whole-hearted bear hug. "Ah, Bree. I couldn't be happier."

He held her at arm's length wearing an ecstatic expression on his face. "You were always my favorite, Breeze my girl," he declared drawing hoots from Skye and Summer.

"You tell each of us the same thing on a random

basis," Skye said.

Mike winked and gave Skye a crooked grin. "And I never lie to any of you."

Still holding Bree loosely, his arms around her shoulders, he gazed down at her. "I can see how you kept the secret from me. But your mother? And your sisters? How did you pull that off?"

"Yeah, how?" Skye realized that had *never* happened to her before.

"I didn't have a single dream. Not one inkling," Summer said.

"I tried something new." Bree's green eyes twinkled with mischief. "I bound a spell to block you all. I wanted to try to surprise you in person."

"I can't believe it," Kay said. "I don't think your aunts and I could ever have done that with each other."

Skye was more than impressed and fascinated at Bree's burgeoning power. Maybe...triplets? She'd have to mull that over for a while.

Kay clasped Bree's hand. "When are you due? Oh, I want to do a baby shower for you. Girls, will you help?"

"Of course."

"You bet."

Kay tilted her head upward squinting in the bright sunshine. "Why are we standing around here? Let's get you out of the sun."

"You must be exhausted from traveling, Bree." Skye reached out her hand. "Let's go sit down on the porch."

"I'll get you a cold drink," Summer said.

"I'll open an umbrella out back. Can I call Karol and Kamille? My sisters will..."

Laughing, Bree held out a hand, stop. "Relax, everyone. Take a breath. Jack sort of went bananas like you are, too, when we found out a couple days ago. Truly, I'm great. Never felt better. And it's *very* early."

Bree didn't resist as Skye towed on her hand anyway. "Come on. We can talk staring at the waves."

"Okay. Mom, of course you can call our aunts. But please caution them. I haven't seen my doctor yet. The whole thing."

Kay clapped her hands together, her green eyes gleaming. "Ooh, I can't wait to tell them."

Summer clasped Bree's free hand and the triplets strolled to the back of the inn. Connected to her sisters, elation surged through Skye like a powerful current. The temptation to burst into flight nearly swamped Skye. How awesome if the tiny life inside Bree might share in the unbridled joy flowing from the Sacred Source.

I'm going to be an aunt! I'm going to be an aunt! "I'm going to be an aunt," she exclaimed. "I'm practically exploding with happiness."

Summer swung Bree's arm back and forth. "Me, too!"

Bree broke free of her sisters' handholds and threw her arms around Skye and Summer instead. "I'm going to have a baby!"

Skye nestled her head against Bree's shoulder. "Uh uh. You're going to have *three* babies."

Bree widened her eyes and beamed at Skye. "Yes, I suppose I might."

The triplets hung in that once in a lifetime embrace beneath a Carolina cornflower blue sky, inhaling deeply the briny scents of the sea, the cooling breeze soft against their skin.

"Want to take a barefoot walk?" Bree loosened the hug. "I'm too antsy to sit."

"Oh yeah." Summer bent at the waist and untied her sneakers.

Bree followed suit.

Skye kicked off her sandals. "Sounds great."

Bree and Summer at her side, Skye waded through drifts of warm sand straight toward the water. Lazy breakers ebbed offshore, rolling in a parade of foaming surf that bubbled wet aprons on the sand. She jumped at the first icy touch of a shallow wave against her ankles and calves. The water temperature of the Atlantic in May, even as far south as North Carolina, still hovered in the low sixties. A couple sloshes later, she acclimated and relished wading in the cool water.

"Is Jack freaked out at the proposition of three babies at once?" Summer said.

Bree shook her head. "Not really. Now, that is. When I first told him our truth and then he witnessed our power during Ella's rescue he had his total freak out."

Her lips twisted in a wry grin. "And then he came to his senses and proposed. He knew what he was getting into. The thing is, we're not sure yet if I'm having triplets."

Skye nodded agreement. "True. But what does your heart tell you?"

Bree stopped short and burst out laughing. "Oh yeah. We're in for it."

They resumed strolling along the sand soaking up the sunshine and the pleasure of the first of many beach walks during coveted sister time. Gulls squawked winging overhead, pelicans fished skimming the waters of cresting waves, and sand pipers skittered in and out just beyond the water's reach ahead of the waves' advance. The roar of the ocean's constant movements filled Skye's ears.

Summer's sweet voice broke through the white noise of sea sounds. "So, when are you going to tell us about him, Skye?"

Him. Skye pulled up short drawing her sisters to a halt on either side of her. "What?"

"Yeah, I'm *really* curious," Bree said. "I've got to say that vision last night was hot, hot, hot."

"I had a steamy dream to say the least," Summer added fanning her face with her hand. "All I have to say is, wow. You two must be having a *fine* time."

Skye gasped at the inuendo. "Oh…no…" she sputtered. "I've never…we've never…"

She spun around ready to flee back down the beach.

Summer clasped Skye's elbow. "Wait. Please."

Her sister's soft gaze held Skye in place. "I'm sorry, Skye. I figured we were clued in on exactly what you saw."

Skye bit the corner of her lower lip. "Well… I guess you were. I *did* see Gabe last night. But…well, not from experience. I mean not in person." She wagged her head. "I'm not making any sense."

Bree touched Skye's arm gently. "We're pretty turned around, too. Sit. I'm so curious about, Gabe, is it?"

Skye nodded, yes, and then followed Bree up to a rise in the sand plopping down next to her on a spot beyond the reach of lapping waves.

Summer sat down beside her putting Skye second in the row of triplets. "First of all, he's gorgeous, Skye. I'd say a possible match worthy of you. What do you think, Bree?"

"Absolutely," Bree chimed in. "I'm so happy for you. Most importantly, whoever he is, he's one lucky man."

"Really?" Skye couldn't believe her ears. Her sisters saw her with Gabe as…a couple? A match?

"I…" Skye didn't know what to say.

"Start wherever, please," Summer urged. "I'm dying to know anything you want to tell us about him."

"Okay. His name is Gabriel Hartley. He's from Virginia, and get this, his granddad left him Mermaid Cottage. It's not too far down the beach from here."

"I know that place."

"Me, too. Wait," Bree said. "Was his grandfather the retired senator?"

"Yes. Gabe's a senator now, too," Skye said.

"Holy shit. I know a lot about him," Summer professed. "He's a Conservative. A little too Republican for my taste. But so far, I can't take issue with what he stands for. He's made a lot of inroads in Washington for a Junior Senator."

"Huh. I'm totally out of the loop about politicians," Skye said. "I didn't know you were political, Summer."

Summer hooted. "Are you kidding? I was an ADA in New York City. I fairly *drowned* in politics."

"Really the most important thing is how Skye views him, right?" Bree said. "Sweetie, is he as fine a person as his *very* fine bod?"

The triplets burst into bawdy laughter.

Enjoying the silliness and good-natured ribbing,

Skye savored her new reality. She never even partially believed that she might share confidences about her love interests with her beloved sisters. And yet, Gabe *was* in her life, and she *was* very interested in love.

Skye rose to her feet, presented her back to the ocean, and gazed down on her sisters. "Come on, let's head back. We have a whole week to talk."

She offered each of her hands to Bree and Summer to tow them to their feet. A flicker of swirling color in the cloudless sky had Skye raising her eyes. "Ooh. They're releasing a group of butterflies at the Elizabethan Gardens."

Skye wiggled her eyebrows at her sisters. "Want to go?"

"Sure."

"Oh, yes!"

Not wasting a second, Skye locked hands with each of her sisters and bound the spell. Three vivid, scarlet butterflies glided the currents to unite with the fluttering cloud of Monarchs.

Chapter 12

Gabe took a bandana out of his back pocket, mopped sweat off his forehead, and surveyed the cargo hold. After a lot of maneuvering, he had managed to squeeze his grandfather's wooden rocking chair into the back of the farm van without a single scratch. He loaded a few more boxes with those of Grandfather's possessions that Gabe thought best permanently belonged at the beach cottage and strode back into the horse barn.

"There's my girl." The jet-black mare whinnied as Gabe approached her stall. The other horses reacted to his voice; but Gabe focused on Ebony Storm, his most-loved horse, in foal for the first time. He hoped he could leave Washington and return to the farm in late spring or early summer whenever she went in to labor.

He stroked Storm's mane fondly. "Don't look at me with those sad eyes. I have to go; but I promise I'll come back soon."

"She's just playing you for a treat. Storm knows a softie when she sees him." Bradley Thompson laughed as he came up behind Gabe and clapped him on the back.

"Hey, Brad. You know I can't resist those eyes." They shook hands. "How is she doing?"

"She's doing great. Doc was here a couple of days ago and is happy with her progress. She's a beauty." Brad petted the mare's muzzle. "I saw the van loaded.

117

You should have called me to help."

"You have enough to do. I'll have it back to you in a couple of days."

"Keep it as long as you need it. Now give the little lady here the apple you have in your pocket. She has been very patient."

Gabe doled out the fruit to Storm as Brad turned to leave.

"Hey Brad?" Gabe called out.

He halted gazing at Gabe. "Yeah?"

"Thank you for taking care of this place and keeping an eye out for Mother."

"No thanks necessary. It's my pleasure and honor. Your grandfather was a great man and…he is sorely missed." His voice caught.

"If you need anything, I'm just a phone call away."

"I wouldn't tear you away from all that important stuff in D.C." Brad winked at him. "But thanks. Noted."

Gabe grabbed a bag of apples and strolled stall to stall handing out treats to each horse. He knew the entire stable by name and personality; some of the horses were friends since he was a young boy. He had spent whole days as a kid working with the hands in the horse barn, training, grooming, and even happily mucking out stalls—and best of all, riding Ebony Storm. Gabe wished that he could spend more time there that day. But Storm was in no condition for him to ride her, and he needed to set out for the beach.

He stopped one last time at Storm's stall and gave her another apple. "After all, you *are* eating for two."

Tossing the empty burlap bag near the barn door on the way out, Gabe jogged back to his house. He picked up the duffle he had left on the porch in his left hand

and fished his cell phone out of his back pocket with his right hand giving the virtual assistant the command to dial Skye. Gabe paced toward the truck.

Continuing their two days running phone tag, he left her a voice mail message. "Hi, it's me again. I'm heading to the Banks today. How about dinner tonight? Give me a call back when you can. Hopefully, I'll see your beautiful face soon."

He pocketed the phone, set the duffle on the passenger seat, rounded the front bumper, swung open the door, sprang into the driver's seat, and fired up the engine.

Twenty minutes later, Gabe zipped through the E-Z Pass lane at the Chesapeake Bay Bridge-Tunnel toll plaza. Driving over the bridge Gabe relaxed rather than tensing up at the horizon blanking view and dizzying height of the twenty-three-mile span, an engineering marvel that had the reputation of the ninth scariest bridge in the world. He basked in the sunshine streaming directly through the truck's windshield. He equated that spot in the drive with lifelong eager anticipation of a beach vacation.

His mind wandered, recalling the times he rode the same route with his granddad, headed for the beach cottage with the car speakers blaring music. His grandfather favored classical instrumentals while driving, but sometimes deferred to Gabe's preference for the country station on the radio.

Gabe's dad died when he was twelve years old. The senator stepped up to fill the father figure role. But Gabe was afraid of his blustery grandfather before Dad's death and for long months afterward. He clearly remembered the night his fear of the powerful man had evaporated.

Granddad had stayed at the ranch instead of returning to Washington after a weekend visit expecting his prized mare to foal. It had begun raining furiously and there were threats of tornadoes when the mare had started the last stage of labor. His grandfather had allowed Gabe to help him until the vet responded to his earlier call—which hadn't happened until well after the mare gave birth. Shoulder to shoulder with Granddad in the stall, he had witnessed the foal's entrance into the world during a brilliant flash of lightning and a booming thunderclap. Gabe still thrilled at the memory.

Granddad had shaken his hand. "You have to name this little filly. She's yours."

Gabe couldn't believe that his grandfather had entrusted a thirteen-year-old boy with such a gift. The foal had a jet-black coat, and her eyes flared with temperament.

"Ebony Storm," Gabe had whispered.

"Great name, boy."

Ebony Storm struggled to stand, fiery determination sparking in her eyes.

"That filly will live up to her name." His grandfather had enveloped him in a hug. The unbreakable bond between Gabe and the senator was born that stormy night.

And now the bond is broken. The first time at the beach cottage without his grandfather in the world would surely be bittersweet.

His phone vibrated against his hip, and he double tapped the AirPod in his right ear answering the call. "Hello, this is Gabe."

"Hello Gabe, this is Skye."

"I'm so glad we finally connected. How are you? How was the visit with your sisters?"

"We had a great time. It went way too fast."

"Good times always do. I'm on the road. Are you free for dinner tonight?"

"I am."

"Wonderful. Are all the restaurants open for the season yet?"

"Most of them are. But I was thinking. I'm sure you'll be tired after unpacking and opening the cottage. We have a ton of food left after my sisters' visit. Would you like me to pack a picnic?"

"That sounds great. I should have everything done by five. Does that work for you?"

"Sure. If you need more time, just text me."

"Skye?"

"Yes?"

"I can't wait to see you."

"Me, too."

Click. She was gone.

He twisted the volume dial to the right. He grinned and then sang along with Garth Brooks.

****

Skye squinted at the acrylic painting appraising her work. "Where did you come from, you pretty girl?"

She had painted the wild horses of Corolla many times, usually for commissions. But this blue-black filly rearing up beneath a gathering bank of storm clouds had sprung fully formed straight from her brush to the canvas. Skye was certain she had never seen the beautiful horse on a North Carolina beach.

"Somebody's going to snap you up." She lifted the canvas off her easel and propped it against the wall lined with paintings that she planned to deliver to the Virginia Beach art gallery.

Skye took a quick shower and then stood in her closet in her underwear. She wished her sisters were there to help her pick something perfect to wear. She dressed, hoping that the white and black, polka dotted maxi skirt paired with a capped sleeve, white crop top that she selected would have met with Bree's and Summer's approval. She twisted her hair up into a loose top knot and let tendrils fall randomly around her face. After a quick brush of mascara and applying a tinted lip gloss, she was ready to go.

Earlier she had asked Mom if she could raid the fridge, explaining that she planned to picnic with "the man I told you about that I met in California." Kay had enthusiastically agreed to Skye's request and had miraculously refrained from grilling Skye for details about Gabe. She wasn't sure why she held back confiding in Mom that Gabe had become important to her. Possibly all important to her. Maybe she just needed to meet him on her own terms—her own turf—and see where that led before a heart to heart with her mother.

When she sidled over to her car parked out in front of the inn, Mike had already loaded a cooler into the passenger seat and wedged another one behind the seat of her Wrangler.

"Two coolers, Dad?"

"I just added a couple bottles of wine to your mother's bounty."

"You guys are the best. Thank you." She stood on tiptoe and bussed his cheek. "Love you."

"Love you too, honey. You know you're my

favorite."

Skye was still laughing as she pulled onto Oregon Inlet Road. Gabe's cottage was a short drive up the beach road. If she didn't have the coolers to contend with, she would have strolled the beach to see him instead.

Set back off the street, Mermaid Cottage stood imposingly at the end of a short driveway. The term "cottage" hardly applied to the stately, weathered wood home. A large window just beneath the pitch of the gabled roof on the north side of the house hinted at an attic room. On the next level down, five windows gleamed on that side and another five windows faced the street. The roof overhung the next floor down creating a sheltered porch that wound around the entire house. Light twinkled reflections in windows behind the stilts on the lowest level. The place made a whopping impression.

Gabe stood at the top of the stairs on the porch. Skye lowered her window and gave him a wave as she braked in a parking spot on the broad gravel apron. Gabe clambered down the wooden steps, his arms stretched wide. She opened her door, slipped out of the car, and was met with an enveloping embrace within Gabe's strong arms, his crisp, cotton shirt warm against her cheek. She sighed softly surrendering to the lovely completeness.

"Finally," he said.

Skye grinned up at him. "I'm not late. It's not even five yet."

He gazed down at her, a mischievous gleam in his eyes. "You know I wasn't referring to the time."

"I brought tons of food. I hope you're hungry."

"I'm starving."

"Great. Can you help carry the coolers?" She edged away from him, but he tightened the embrace holding her in place.

"I thought you were starving."

"You know I wasn't referring to food." He fused his lips to hers, deepening the kiss, lingering, smoldering; Skye didn't want him to stop the pulse racing connection.

She closed her eyes adrift on the eddy of attraction he stirred. When he ended the kiss, she slowly opened her eyes.

He beamed at her, a sexy wicked glint in his eyes. "That's better." Gabe released the embrace.

"Much," she agreed. "I'll get one cooler. Can you carry the other?"

He heaved a cooler out of the front seat. "Just put that one on top, and I'll bring them both inside."

Skye tugged on a handle, lugged the second cooler out from behind the seat, and balanced it in Gabe's arms. She followed him up the long staircase, stopping to check out the porch. Wide wicker rocking chairs with aqua colored pillows stenciled with mermaids lined the interior perimeter.

Gabe set the coolers down near the front door and swung open the screen door. "Come on. I want to show you something."

He took her hand and led Skye into the spacious home. Gabe gave her hand a squeeze as she halted in place taking in her surroundings surprised by the burst of colors inside the house.

Three walls were painted pastel, seafoam green. The entire back wall of the house, directly in front of her, was a massive stretch of glass. The perfect, unobstructed ocean view incorporated the ever-moving sea directly into the huge great room. Thickly cushioned, beige couches with assorted multi-colored throw pillows faced the glass wall. To her right, large, light blue upholstered barrel chairs flanked the floor to ceiling, stone fireplace. A massive TV screen was mounted over the carved oak mantel. To her left stood a white dining room table with matching chairs. Skye counted twenty.

He pointed to the buffet over which hung her painting of three fishermen. "Doesn't it look great there? Like you created it exactly for that spot. I know my grandfather would approve."

She nodded. "I like it there. A lot."

Gabe went back outside and brought in the coolers. He gave a nod toward the back of the house. "Can you get that sliding door for me?"

Skye hustled ahead of him, slid open the slider, and followed Gabe out onto the back deck around to the side porch. A white linen-covered table for two was set with beautiful gold-rimmed china, gold flatware, and gleaming crystal goblets. A three-wicked, white candle in a hurricane lamp was surrounded by a ring of jasmine blossoms that perfumed the breeze.

"My goodness, everything looks lovely." She bent and inhaled the flowers' sweet fragrance. "This is my favorite smell." She gazed up at him.

"I know. It's mine now, too."

The loving expression in his eyes touched her. The perfect thing to say, she thought.

"I wanted our first dinner here to be memorable." He kissed her cheek softly. "Ready to eat?"

Each of them took the lids off the coolers and set out the picnic. When Skye was done, she surveyed the container-laden tabletop. "I guess Mom got a little carried away."

He chuckled. "Good thing I'm hungry."

She took a seat at the table, sweeping a napkin onto her lap and watching him light the candle, uncork a bottle of wine, and fill their glasses.

Gabe sat across from her and raised his glass. "I want to propose a toast to Mark and Lynn. If they didn't get married, we would never have met. I owe them so much."

Skye lifted her glass. "And I would like to toast Sharon."

"Sharon?"

"Yes. If she didn't jilt you, you never would have ambush-kissed me at the rehearsal dinner."

Gabe burst out laughing. "Ambush? I guess that's a good way to put it. Okay. Here's to Mark, Lynn, *and* Sharon."

They clinked glasses, and Skye took a sip of the delicious wine. *Thanks, Dad.*

"Who knew that getting jilted would turn out to be the best thing that ever happened to me?" He reached across the table and gave her hand a squeeze.

Skye's heart leaped. Meeting Gabe seemed to be the best thing that had ever happened to her, too.

Gabe tucked into the food, and Skye helped herself to her favorites—which was just about everything on the table. Over the sumptuous dinner and frequent pours of wine, they talked about their families and their careers.

"Guess what, Gabe? I'm going to be an aunt!"

He clasped her hand across the table. "That's wonderful. Bree, I take it, is the expectant mom?"

"She is. We're all over the moon."

"I'll bet."

"She's due in late December, early January. Who knows? We might have a Christmas baby."

"That's pretty special."

Skye delighted in his warmth, loving his sense of humor, family loyalty, and dedication to his job. He had overcome deep sadness at the loss of his dad as a boy and the recent loss of his grandfather, who was a second father to him, by cherishing every memory of them. This cottage figured a great deal in his store of happy memories with his granddad, and she felt honored to be here with him.

Just the masculine timbre of his voice sent sensual shimmers through her. She thrilled at the possibility that she might mean as much to him as he increasingly meant to her.

The sun set below the fire-streaked horizon and a sickle moon rose. Candlelight flickered between them. She slapped her arm.

"Mosquitoes?"

"Yep."

They rose from the table and made quick work of restowing food containers in the coolers and stacking the dishes. After a few trips back and forth from outside into the kitchen toting dishes, cutlery, glasses, and the coolers, Skye finished storing leftovers in the stainless steel, double-doored fridge and then turned on the faucet filling the sink.

Chapter 13

Gabe came up behind her. "Leave those. I'll take care of them later." He nuzzled the back of her neck.

She shut off the water and leaned back against the hard plane of his chest. His large hands moved up the sides of her arms and over her shoulders massaging lightly. His fingers extended downward provocatively near the swell of her breasts.

Her chest heaved as he ran his hands over her breasts caressing her. She turned to face him draping her arms around his neck. He kissed her, softly, at first, but she needed...more, and she fused her lips hungrily with his. Melting in his arms Skye pressed her body fully against him, floating in a sea of sensations. Her heart raced as heat gathered in her core.

His fingers inched under the hem of her crop top sending electric shivers through her at his touch on her bare skin.

"Silk," he whispered.

Her knees went rubbery, and her nipples hardened as his thumbs stroked her breasts through her bra.

"Stay with me tonight," he whispered against her ear. He cupped her breasts with his hands.

His invitation hit her like a splash of cold water. The night? She froze.

He must have read her body language because he rapidly took his hands off her. "Skye?"

"I can't..." Her breath caught in her throat. "I

128

never…"

She spun on her heel. "I need to leave."

Impulse had her grabbing an empty cooler by the handle in each hand and fleeing the kitchen. She stopped to awkwardly slide open the glass door, step back outside, descend the stairs onto the sand, and veer right intending to circle around the house to where she had parked her car.

"Skye, wait," he shouted from behind her.

Feeling foolish and guilty, she halted in her tracks and turned to face him.

He caught up to her in three long strides, stopping a couple feet away. "I'm sorry if I moved too fast. Please forgive me."

How could she explain that she was terrified to want him so much? Would he understand her complicated reasons to be so afraid?

"It's okay. It isn't you, it's…" Skye trailed off, too overwhelmed by how close she had come to complete abandon of her senses.

"Can I see you to your car?"

"That's all right, Gabe. I'm good. Thank you for this evening."

"You're welcome. Thank your mother for the food. You're sure you're all right?"

"Really. I'll call you tomorrow."

"Promise?"

"Promise."

"Then…goodnight, Skye." He turned back toward the steps trudging slowly through the sand.

When he stopped and gazed out at the ocean, her breath caught on a gasp as she recognized the exact composition of her painting of the dark-headed boy that she had created long ago and sold recently in California. The little boy, now a man, was Gabe.

****

Skye overshot the gravel driveway leading to the inn, consumed with confusion. She barely registered the Jeep's headlights beaming pale lemon on the black macadam in front of the car, autopiloting the deserted beach road. Had she seen Gabe outside Mermaid Cottage when she was a kid? She *had* started creating art at an early age, but she had finished that painting a few years ago. Why had the Sacred Source "sent" an image of Gabe when he was a boy to her canvas years before she had met the grown man?

A tremor ran through her at the possible meaning of the mystery. Was he destined for Skye? While she had enjoyed the normal pleasures of meeting and getting to know a compelling, gorgeous male, her far from normal reality since birth had seemingly insinuated Gabriel Hartley into her life story before she knew the man existed.

What role was Gabe destined to play? Everything she had learned about him, including his tantalizing impetuousness giving her that first kiss, pointed to a fateful connection. If he hadn't dramatically taken the lead, would shy and inexperienced Skye Layton have even allowed a connection? Probably not. Surely, he was meant to draw her out of her protective armor but to what end? True love for her against what she had always considered longshot odds? Could she trust this man enough to strip away her defenses and reveal her true self? There was so much more at stake for Skye than her virginity, although that alone was no small thing. Her soul mate had to, above all, learn *all* about the legend, wholeheartedly accept her extraordinary role with her sisters, *and* tell nothing to no one.

What in the world am I doing getting tangled up with a public figure like Gabe whose private life is picked apart every day?

But she *was* entangled with Gabe, and her heart longed to stay that way.

Her aimless drive led her to a favorite scenic spot along the shore. She pulled off the road and parked in the empty, sand dusted lot. Salt-bleached, wood stairs led to a narrow boardwalk on the top of a steep dune. She left the car, climbed the stairs, and picked her way along the wood slats to the crest of the dune. Standing beneath a magnificent, glittering celestial dome, she wrapped her arms around her torso and gazed at the panorama of starry night and moonlit sea. The breeze whipped her face unfurling more tendrils from her updo. Skye blanked her mind and silenced her internal monologue. Here she might not find answers, but she could always find her Sacred Source at the beach.

Movement in the corner of her left eye redirected her gaze. A shooting star streaked a brilliant trail in the blue-black sky. "Oh!"

Skye grinned the entire three seconds that the display blazed in the sky. When the star fizzled out like spent fireworks, she felt baptized with blessing and peace.

"Thank you," she said to the heavens.

Turning toward the staircase, Skye retraced her steps along the boardwalk, back to the car, and headed home.

Braking beneath a copse of palm trees in her accustomed space out front of The Inn of the Three

Butterflies, she noticed the glow of the parlor lamp in a first-floor window. Her dashboard digital display read 12:10. Way past her parents' usual bedtime.

They waited up for me.

Even though just about a month away from celebrating her thirty-second birthday, Skye tiptoed up the front steps and unlatched the front door noiselessly like a sneaky teen violating curfew. She treaded softly inside the house inhaling the fresh baked cookie scents which always perfumed her home.

"Skye?" came Kay's soft voice.

She stepped around the partition wall between the vestibule and front parlor and stood within the archway. Kay perched in the corner of the vintage sofa with her legs curled under her, a hardcover book open in her lap. The lamp reflected a soft halo of reddish light around her crown of auburn hair. She took off her reading glasses and beamed at Skye. "Did you have a nice evening?"

"I did…um, yes… I hope it's all right. I gave Gabe all the leftovers."

"Of course, it's all right." Kay narrowed her eyes and pinned Skye with a classic maternal is-that-all-you-have-to-say-for-yourself fixed look.

Skye shifted from one foot to the other. Of course, she trusted her mom with the secrets of her heart. Skye's heart was under siege, and she didn't know how to manage the turbulence. "I left the coolers in the car. I'll bring them inside in the morning."

"Uh huh." Kay crossed her arms over her chest.

"Um. Are you too tired to talk for a while, Mom?"

Kay patted the cushion next to her and put her book on the end table in answer.

Skye scurried to her mother's side, now eager to unburden her confusion.

"Do you want to tell me about your...date tonight?" Kay said.

"I think I want to start before that."

"I'm listening, sweetheart."

"Well. You know I was kind of thrown together with Gabe at Lynn's wedding. He has a similar history with Lynn's new husband as I do with her, and he was the Best Man. We first met at the elaborate rehearsal dinner at a country club. Black tie and all that. He looked *extremely* handsome in a tux. It was a bit unconventional right from the start."

"What was?"

"How I first met him. He kind of grabbed hold of me and kissed me stupid."

"*What?* Honey, I'm glad your dad is already in bed. I'm pretty sure he would not be happy hearing that."

Skye huffed a laugh. "It's a long story, but he wanted to really impress on his former fiancée, whom he didn't expect to be at the dinner and who jilted him for another man, that he had definitely moved on."

"I trust he made his point. Did you slap him silly?"

She burst out laughing. "Honestly, Mom, it was the best first kiss I could ever imagine. Truly, he's a gentleman in every way." Her stomach sank thinking about how abruptly she had rebuffed him without any explanation after a beautiful, romantic evening.

"He proved that tonight." A hot blush bloomed on Skye's face remembering his tantalizing touch, the taste of his lips, the thrall of his strong arms around her, how he honored her sudden and unexplained—no. And how deep down she didn't want him to stop.

Kay arched her eyebrows but didn't probe. She folded her hands in her lap and waited.

Skye was a relationship novice. She had listened avidly to her sisters' opposite sex woes and triumphs over the years relishing the girl talk, providing encouragement, and sometimes devising distraction from her sisters' heartbreaks. But she had little to offer the sisterhood from personal experience. Skye had had her share of prom and homecoming dates, a couple of girlhood crushes and go nowhere dates with a few men. Period.

Even though her identical sisters' love and advice meant everything to Skye, especially since both Bree and Summer had found their soul mates, she had held back with them regarding Gabe. Her emotions were a pretzel knot. How could she unravel them when the thought of him filled her with both yearning and terror at the same time?

"I guess I'm not doing a very good job of explaining, am I?" Skye peered at Kay hoping that her mother's ability to "see" with uncanny clarity might spare her from trying to express what bothered her when she wasn't sure herself.

"You can tell me anything you want, sweetheart. I promise two things: I won't judge, and I'm on your side."

"Thanks, Mom. I know that. It's just…I think this man is important. Very important. And I don't know how to trust my feelings for him. Do you think I'm making him into mister right just because Bree and Summer are so happy? And he seems like he's taken with me?"

"I don't know how to answer that except to say you need to follow your heart. You'll know. If you feel deeply that he's the man who is meant for you, why question that?"

"Because I can't have that."

"Why on earth not?"

"I'm like Aunt Karol, right, Mom?"

"Yes, I guess. You're paramount of the triplets, like her." She huffed. "If anything, I think you possess greater power."

"You see?" Skye sat on the edge of the sofa. "She never got married because she couldn't let any man have that power over her or the legend."

"Oh, that's not true at all." Kay clasped both of Skye's hands. "Karol's choices are hers alone. The legend has survived because the Sacred Source prevails. It's important not to underestimate that. Or overestimate your own powers."

Skye nodded her head. "I get that. But... Is the Sacred Source ever wrong?"

"What?" Kay arched her eyebrows. "I've never even flirted with that question. Why would you ask that?"

"Do you remember the painting I did of a boy on the beach near Mermaid Cottage?"

Kay furrowed her brow. "No. I don't think so."

"I finished it a few years ago and included it in the work I sent to California for the showings."

"All right." Kay gazed at her intently.

"Gabe recently inherited Mermaid Cottage from his grandfather. We had dinner there tonight. I left him on the beach when I ended the evening. I turned around and glimpsed him walking on the sand. Mom. The painting I did was him. He must have been around ten years old or so."

Kay threw her arms around Skye. "Oh, sweetheart. I'm so happy for you! What more could you ask of the Sacred Source? I believe you should set aside any misgivings and trust that your path is clear."

"Really?" Skye bit the corner of her lip.

"You're still not convinced?"

"Mom, he's a senator. A *very* public figure."

"He is?"

"Uh huh. Gabriel Hartley from Virginia."

"Oh…" Kay narrowed her eyes. "I know who he is. I don't think I've ever heard anything negative about him. That's kind of amazing given he's a politician."

"Honestly, I never heard of him before we met. And when it comes to politics, I don't know a whole lot more about him now. But Mom. I think I'm already falling in love with him. Asking him to keep my brand of secrets? I must be crazy."

"You want me to look."

Skye exhaled, relieved. "Would you?"

Kay unfolded her legs and swung them over the edge of the sofa. She planted her feet firmly on the ground and straightened in her seat closing her eyes.

Nervous energy had Skye's heels tapping against the oak floor as she watched her mother. Kay's neck arched and she remained immobile for what felt like minutes to Skye.

When Kay blinked open her eyes a slow smile curled on her lips. She laid her warm hand on Skye's arm. "I see nothing but good in him."

Skye's heart somersaulted. "Really? You're sure?"

"I'm sure."

"Thank you, Mom. I love you."

Kay wrapped her arm around Skye and drew her closer. "I love you, too, sweetheart."

Chapter 14

Moonbeams cast a shimmering blanket on the waves crashing below her perch. Skye propped her legs up on the railing of the small balcony off her penthouse studio mulling over Mom's opinion of Gabe. *He doesn't pose a threat.* Kay's gift of flawless insight freed Skye's heart to open to the possibility of loving him if…

Her phone vibrated in her pocket. Skye's pulse raced knowing before she looked at the screen that Gabe was calling.

She answered rapidly, eager for the chance to explain why she hadn't stayed with him longer that night. "Gabe, I…"

"Forgive me, Skye. I know you promised to call me tomorrow, but I couldn't wait until then." His deep throated chuckle rumbled in her ear. "I miss you already and, honestly, I was afraid you might not call at all."

Guilt pinched Skye. "Oh, Gabe. I'm sorry if I led you to believe that you did something wrong. You didn't. Forgive me for running off on you?"

"Pretty lady, as long as you let me catch you, I'm good."

She threw back her head and laughed, delighted that he joked away any tension between them.

"Can I see you tomorrow? In the morning I'm going to check on my grandfather's boat. Feel like going for a boat ride?"

"I'd love to. What time? I have something to do first thing, but I should be back home by eight. Want me to meet you at the marina?"

"No need. I'll pick you up at eight."

"Okay. See you tomorrow then."

"Can't come too soon. Good night, Skye."

"Night, Gabe."

She floated inside and got ready for bed. Skye burrowed under the soft, cotton sheets and curled onto her side, her hand under her pillow beneath her cheek. She was asleep in minutes and didn't stir until four thirty when her body clock woke her.

Rested and alert, Skye bounced out of bed and slipped on white, terry shorts, donned her bright teal, N.E.S.T. T-shirt, and twisted her hair up to tuck under a baseball cap. She hurried down the stairs, moving quietly through the first-floor hallways, eased out the front door, and slipped behind the wheel of her Jeep.

Within ten minutes, Skye arrived at the patrol point down the beach from the inn. She swung her leg over the saddle of one of the ATVs and greeted the other driver next to her. They started their machines and headed off in different directions on the beach.

Skye didn't locate any new turtles' nests during her patrol. She returned to the vehicles' access point, parked the ATV, and then drove back to the inn looking forward to heading straight into the shower. She was dressed and ready to go by seven forty-five. Sitting on the front deck in happy anticipation, she sipped lemon tea from a Brew-thru travel mug on the lookout for Gabe. A satchel packed with a sketch pad, a few bottles of water, and sunscreen leaned against her leg. She felt his arrival before the white truck pulled onto the driveway apron.

Gabe braked, threw open the door, and hopped out of the truck. His raven hair glinted in the early morning sun. He wore tailored navy-blue shorts and a torso-hugging, crimson POLO T-shirt. The hem of each short sleeve ringed bulging biceps. Just the sight of him was pure pleasure.

She rose and skipped down the front stoop.

"Good morning, beautiful." He opened his arms heading directly toward her.

Skye met him on the gravel driveway in a couple of strides. He enveloped her in a hug. She nestled her head against his solid chest inhaling his clean scent.

He kissed her crown and then loosened his hold on her gazing down into her eyes. "Are you okay riding in that old van? I forgot I didn't have my car when I said I'd pick you up."

"Of course, I am. Why not?"

"Well. Most of the women I cross paths with wouldn't be caught dead in it."

"Really? Prissy if you ask me."

Gabe grinned. "Yeah. Stuck up."

He turned toward the truck and draped his arm over her shoulders.

Skye strolled at Gabe's side to the passenger door and halted. He opened the door for her and then angled an elbow so she could brace against his forearm for balance climbing up into her seat. Simply touching him sent a rush of shivers through her. Inside, country music played low on the radio.

Gabe drove over the bridge on the way to the marina.

She took in the view of aquamarine water, pearly sand, and pelicans flying in formation over the dunes. "Where do you dock your boat?"

"You mean my grandfather's boat. Uh..." He wagged his head. "Haven't fully accepted it's my boat now. Grandad always used Harley's dockyard. I don't see any reason to change. Do you know Harley?"

"I sure do. Harley and my dad have been friends for years. We've spent childhood summers with his boys, Jake and Ryan. Do you know them?"

"Not well. I've met them a few times. They seem nice."

"Good people. Growing up, they were like the brothers we never had, so we fought a lot. Typical boys, they knew the right way to do everything." She chuckled. "We taught them otherwise many times."

"I can just imagine." He reached over and squeezed her knee, his warm touch soothing and possessive.

Skye covered his hand with hers and was content to rest it there for the remainder of the drive.

Pickup trucks filled Harley's parking lot leaving only a few open spaces for Gabe to use.

"Busy here," he said.

"It's like this every day once the season starts." Skye opened her door and slid out of her seat.

Gabe met her around the rear of the truck clasping her hand for the walk to the office. Before they reached the entrance, Harley burst through the doorway on a bead for Skye.

The bear-like man wrapped her in a hug and reared back swooping Skye a couple inches off the ground. He swung her back down and then held her at arm's length. "What a wonderful surprise. You, lass, are a sight for sore eyes."

He shifted his attention to Gabe widening his eyes when Gabe put his arm around Skye's shoulders. "Good to see you too, son. How are you doing?" He patted Gabe on the side of his arm. "We lost a great man. He will be missed."

"Yes. Thank you for coming to the funeral."

"He was my friend. I couldn't stay away."

No mistaking the pain written on both men's faces.

Skye shaded her eyes with a hand over her brow gazing out at the Sound. "Looks like a beautiful day to be out on the water," she said lightly, hoping to dispel the dark shadows of mourning.

"I thought we could take grandfather's boat out if it's summer ready," Gabe said.

"Let's go have a look. Jake was working on it last night when I left."

"Did I hear my name?" Jake approached them wiping his hands on a rag. "Hey, Gabe. Good to see you."

Jake shook hands with Gabe but focused directly on Skye. "What brings you here?"

"I'm going out with Gabe on his boat."

Jake burst out laughing. "You *do* know that Gabe's boat is a fishing boat, right?"

Gabe knit his brows at Jake's amusement.

"Behave yourself, Jake," Harley said. "Is the boat ready for a run?"

"I had to change out the carburetor and was just about to take it for a quick test run. "

"Is it okay if we tag along?" said Gabe. "I haven't taken the boat out by myself for years, and I could look over your shoulder as you pilot."

"Okay with you, Pops?" Jake said.

"Sure. Take the day off if you like. Go have fun. It's a beautiful day."

"I'll grab some gear for you." Jake strode away.

****

Free of its moorings, the boat skimmed the water streaming a frothy wake. Skye lazed in one of the two jumbo fishing club chairs facing aft as Gabe and Jake co-piloted through the Oregon Inlet. They passed under the new Basnight Bridge. Her sketch pad lay unopened on Skye's lap. She leaned back her head against the padded headrest and closed her eyes.

Peace pervaded Skye's senses on the water unlike anywhere on land. The waves rocking the boat lulled her into grogginess. She must have dozed because when she opened her eyes Gabe sat next to her with a fishing pole clasped tightly between his hands furiously cranking the reel against a taught line. She scooted up straight in the chair. Jake leaned against the railing smirking and gazing directly into Skye's eyes.

"It's a big one, Jake." Gabe rose to his feet, exerting counter force with the pole taking steps closer to the railing, reeling in the line more and more rapidly. Still, the fish opposed him.

"What do you think I've hooked?" Gabe said.

Jake moved next to him when he reached the rail. "Probably a red drum. How's that for beginner's luck?" He slapped Gabe on the back. "Good eats tonight."

"I had blackened Cajun red drum last year in New Orleans. Blew me away it was so good." Gabe grunted as he tugged the fish closer to the boat. "Can't wait to fillet this baby."

Skye's anger mounted as the men worked in

143

tandem and hauled the beautiful fish onto the deck of the boat.

Gabe swiped sweat off his forehead with palm of his hand. "How big do you think he is?"

Jake backed up, his cell phone in hand pointing the lens at Gabe and his trophy. "Has to be about fifty pounds." He squinted into the viewfinder, snapped the shot, and then ambled over to Gabe and showed him the screen.

"What do you think you're doing?" Skye rose and rushed toward them, furious with herself for dozing through the travesty. If she were alert when Gabe had cast his reel, she would have steered all the fish away from the boat and have saved this poor boy this trauma.

Both men raised their heads and gaped at her.

"Unhook him immediately and put him right back in his home," she demanded.

Her hands trembled as she knelt next to the bucking fish.

"Oh, here we go," Jake growled. "I knew this was too good to be true. Don't say I didn't warn you, buddy."

"What do you mean you warned him?" Skye clasped her hands in front of her to stop their trembling.

"Calm down, sweetheart." Jake said. "I told him how you were a jinx when you were a kid and we never wanted to go out fishing with you."

Gabe apparently was more interested in making Skye feel better than coveting his trophy fish. He stooped down and carefully removed the hook. He gave Jake a head nod as he slipped his forearms underneath the catch's still wriggling body.

Jake sauntered over at the implied request, bent

down to position on Gabe's opposite side, lifted in unison with him, and then toted the fish up over the railing of the boat and into the water.

Skye hung over the railing, satisfied that she had intervened just in time.

Gabe wrapped an arm around her shoulders. "You okay?"

She stood erect and gazed up at him. "Now I am. Thank you."

"I guess you don't catch fish?"

"Ha!" Jake snorted. "That's an understatement. Never met a bigger jinx."

"I *never* wanted to fish, Jake. You know that about me," she fired back.

"Jinx."

"You sound like a five-year old," she retorted.

"Same to you." Jake stalked back to the wheel.

Gabe squeezed her shoulder. "I don't think you're a jinx. I wish you told me that you don't like fishing, though. I would never have asked you to come."

"I'm sorry. I shouldn't have made such a scene." She snuggled closer to him, nestling her head against his shoulder, shaken that she hadn't prevented the whole episode.

"You call that a scene? I've seen a *lot* worse on the Senate floor."

She gazed up at him feeling embarrassed and justified at the same time.

"I can tell you're really upset. Tell me why. I want to understand." He led her gently to a club chair and then sat down next to her.

Skye gazed out at the waves. "When I swam in the ocean from as far back as I could remember I sensed all the fish and sea life around me. I considered them friends. I even named them and imagined their peaceful lives living in the ocean, and the families they made."

She hesitated just short of relating that she had started to communicate with marine life, and they with her, when she was just a toddler. Jake wasn't wrong about her jinxing a successful catch. Skye had purposely warned away all the fish from his dad's encroaching boat, kind of like sending out a sonar alert.

Since Jake and his brother had never caught a single fish when she was aboard, aggravating them no end, she had learned that she was very good at sending out the "swim away" alert. So good that eventually no one had caught a single fish off the Banks.

The commercial and sport fishermen community had been in an uproar. Her dad had figured out that Skye was responsible after another outing with Harley and his boys. During that trip he had caught her moving her lips in silent interlocution perched on the bow. That night Mike had insisted on speaking with her after dinner and had asked her point blank if she had anything to do with the lack of fish in Outer Banks' waters.

At first, she had hedged and said she knew for a fact that there were zillions of fish in the water. He had gently pressed her to tell the truth, and she had admitted that she had warned the fish away whenever she saw a fishing boat heading out. He had calmly explained that some people made their living fishing and, though she was a vegan, not everyone saw the world the same way that she did.

He had promised that she didn't have to go fishing with him, the family, or any of their friends anymore, but she needed to promise him in return to stop ruining the fishing industry. She had agreed. But she had still wanted to sound the alert when she spied a fishing boat offshore.

"The fish are actually my friends now, too, Gabe. I know, I'm crazy." Skye didn't dare look at him, positive that he was rolling his eyes.

"I don't think you're crazy at all. I think you're adorable." Gabe kissed her cheek softly.

She gazed at him in wonder, amazed at his easy acceptance.

"But…I had planned to dazzle you with a fresh caught dinner tonight, so now you have to figure out where we'll eat instead."

"Thank you…" *For not questioning. Could you truly accept who I really am?*

"Are your sisters like you? Do they talk to fish?" He grinned at her, pretty adorable himself with his dancing eyes, chiseled features, and sexy dimples on his cheeks.

"No." She wagged her head. "When you say it out loud, I do sound crazy. Jake and Ryan loved when Summer went out with them, even though she caught the biggest fish every time. You would have had a much better time with Summer today."

"Oh, I don't think so. I'm perfectly happy with the sister who makes friends with fish." He gently tugged her to her feet and drew her toward him in one fluid movement into a lip lock.

The seascape disappeared, and Skye was spellbound by the magic only Gabe could perform.

Chapter 15

Gabe reluctantly loosened his arms around Skye and ended the kiss, tempted to let his hands roam over her luscious body. Clad only in a tank top and thigh skimming shorts, Skye's jasmine scented nearness was a constant challenge to his restraint. But hold back he would, fully intending to let her take the lead beyond hugs and kissing. The last thing Gabe wanted to do was to send her running again.

He led her to the railing to enjoy the ride back to the marina, content to let Jake captain solo, and maybe cool off after the fishing incident. Gabe was happy just to be with her, his arm draped loosely over her shoulder. Skye's profile captivated him. Her fair skin; her sparkling pine green eyes; her glorious, shining mane of silky, russet hair; the curve of her breast; slim waist; and long, long legs tantalized him. That body. The memory of her softness under his hands had him fantasizing about shedding clothes and immersing in that softness. God, he wanted her.

But he'd go slow as long as she needed rather than scare her away again. Skye fascinated him with seeming contradictions. She was shy but poised, sweet but genuine, innocent but a temptress. And there was something more about her, an undercurrent of feminine power both mysterious and magnetizing—like a fire that smoldered beneath the surface that if stoked fully would burn too hot to touch. Gabe had never felt more ready to walk into the flames.

She turned her attention away from the waves, sun, and sky, and gazed up at him. "Beautiful out on the water, isn't it?"

He held her gaze. "Absolutely beautiful."

Skye smiled sweetly; he hoped because she caught his double meaning.

"I've been thinking about places to go for dinner. I have a suggestion that's definitely off the beaten path if you're up for it," she said.

"Anywhere you want is fine with me, as long as steak is on the menu. You're not friends with any cows, are you?"

"No cows around here that I know of. Horses, however, are a different story."

"I'd like to think horses are my friends, too. Would never eat 'em." He shuddered at the thought. "Where do you want to go for dinner?"

"Well...the place I have in mind doesn't have any meat on the menu. It's one hundred percent vegan."

"Oh, of course. I'm sorry I forgot. Let me rephrase. Anywhere you want to go is fine with me."

"Are you sure? I could order a roasted vegetables plate at The Char House."

"I'm sure. I want to take you to your favorite restaurant."

"I do love this restaurant. It's called Senza Facce Ristorante."

"Italian?"

"Uh huh." She giggled. "Translated, it means No Faces Restaurant."

"I don't get it."

"Vegans might say that they won't eat anything

with a face."

He snorted. "Ugh. That's kind of awful. I don't like to think of my food having had a face."

"Right? I'll make a vegan out of you yet. It's little more than a shack tucked away on an inlet. The owners are throwbacks to the sixties. Mom always, very fondly, referred to them as crunchy granola. The food is delicious, and I love everything on the menu. Whenever I got to choose a restaurant for family nights out, this was it. Plus, they have a little outdoor patio that faces west."

She pointed to the sky. "We should see a pretty sunset in a couple hours from there with all those low clouds on the horizon. Sound good?"

"Sounds great." He wrapped her in his arms as Jake brought the boat dockside.

And then he and Skye launched into action to help Jake anchor and secure the moorings.

Jake's eyes danced as he held out a hand to Skye. She took hold and hopped off the boat onto the wooden dock. "Remind me not to go out fishing with you again," he said.

She tapped the side of his arm playfully. "No chance of that. See ya, Jake."

Seated in the passenger seat of the van, Skye bent over her phone. Her thumbs rapidly tapped the keyboard. A swish sounded. "I texted Senza Facce. They don't take reservations, but locals in the know get preferential treatment."

"Good. Do we need to change first?"

"Nope. Dress around here is shorts and flipflops just about everywhere."

"All right, then. Where am I heading?"

"Back to Croatan Highway and then I'll direct you from there."

Several groups congregated on benches and at a lone picnic table outside the restaurant where Gabe steered off the road into the parking area. "Looks like there's a wait."

Skye opened her door. "No, there won't be. Come on."

He walked next to Skye to the front entrance. Gabe held open the door for her and followed her inside squinting in the dimness contrasted to the bright sunshine outside.

"Hey, Flora." Skye addressed a short, squat woman with boyishly cut salt and pepper hair dressed in a tropical print muumuu. "Can we go out to the table?"

"Sure thing, honey." She handed Skye and Gabe legal size, paper menus. "I'll send Ned out to take your order in a few."

"Thanks."

He trailed Skye as she headed toward the back of the small, packed space toward a door. She turned the knob, walked halfway through the threshold, and then held the door open for him until he placed his hand on the door behind her.

Gabe followed her to the only table on the wood deck, which was built on pilings above a cove of the Sound. He held the chair back for her and then moved her seat closer to the table before he took his place across from her. "This is great. Flora gave you the full celebrity treatment."

She grinned at him. "How do you know it isn't because you're a big deal senator?"

He delighted at the mischievous glint in her eyes.

"Because she, and no one else, for that matter, didn't even glance at me. I think that was all about a big deal artist."

Skye wagged her head. "I don't think Flora has a clue about art. She just loves her locals."

"Pretty spot." He scanned the scenery and relaxed in the soft breeze, relishing the prospect of discovering more about her by spending another evening with Skye. Who knows? One day, hopefully soon, they might spend the night together discovering everything about each other. Where there's a will…

His view of her was obstructed as she held the menu up in front of her face. Gabe scanned his menu, also. "Any recommendations?"

She put down the menu on the table. "Well, everything is great and made in house: cheese ravioli, vegetable lasagna, pasta Alfredo…"

"What are you ordering?"

"I'm addicted to the rigatoni pasta with lentil Bolognese sauce."

"Seriously? Lentils? I don't know."

"If you normally like Bolognese, trust me, you'll love this."

"All right, lentils it is."

She placed their identical orders with a stubby gentleman who wore a tropical print, short-sleeved shirt with a starched white apron tied around his ample waist—Flora's Ned, Gabe presumed—a perfect example of spouses who looked like opposite sex versions of each other.

Ned placed a basket of bread and a custard cup of butter on the table and then spun around toward the restaurant.

"Sir? Ned, is it?" Gabe said.

"Yes." Ned turned to face the table.

"Can we please have a bottle of Barolo, also?"

"Sure thing."

"So," Gabe said passing the basket of bread to Skye. "What do you like to do besides paint and fend off kissing attacks from men like me."

"Senator Hartley, no one has ever attack-kissed me before you." Her eyes danced. "And if I recall, I didn't particularly fend you off."

"Yes, that's right. I'm a lucky man."

She passed him the basket and then spread butter on her bread, her eyes downcast. Such a lovely face, he thought. Skye took a dainty bite, and he fixated on her lips. Every graceful move that she made insinuated sensuality to him.

He selected a slice of bread from the basket feeling suddenly ravenous.

"You look beautiful, Skye. I've been meaning to tell you that all day."

Her cheeks blushed pinkish, and she raised a hand to tuck a tendril of hair behind her ear. "Thank you," she said casting her gaze downward at herself. "But I'm hardly dressed to deserve the compliment."

"There hasn't been a minute that you haven't deserved the compliment no matter what you wore."

Her soulful eyes bored into his. They hung in each other's thrall as time seemed to stand still and the setting sun cast a citrus-colored halo around her head. If Ned hadn't bustled through the door and brought plates of food over to their table, Gabe surely would have arched over the tabletop and attack-kissed her squarely on those soft lips.

"Thanks, Ned," she said. "This looks delicious. Gabe, taste it and see what you think."

Gabe picked up his fork and sampled a rigatoni drenched in sauce. "I like it. Not that I'm a big lentils fan, but I do like this. Thanks for the recommendation."

She gave him a sunny smile and a nod, and then dug into the food. Gabe ate, too, the plant-based "meat" sauce growing on him with each forkful. He took a sip of water and then realized that they'd yet to receive the bottle of wine he had ordered. Slipping his napkin off his lap, he placed it on the table and shoved back his chair a couple feet.

Skye glanced up at him.

"I'm going to go find Ned and that bottle of wine."

"Oh. Okay," she said.

He rose from his seat, and a text tone sounded. Gabe halted to read the notification. "Change of plans if you're game. Want to have that bottle of wine at Mermaid Cottage? I hope we'll have a treat in store in an hour or so."

Gabe stepped behind her and grasped the back of her chair.

She arched her neck looking up at him, knitting her brows, but put her napkin on her plate and let him pull her chair away from the table. Skye clasped his outstretched hand and stood up. Gabe led her back into the restaurant, to the cash register to settle the bill, and then out into the lot.

"Who texted you to make you decide to leave so suddenly?" she said, buckling her seatbelt in the truck.

"NASA."

Skye did a double take. "Seriously."

"NASA. Seriously." He steered the truck out of the

154

lot and merged onto the one lane road.

"Wow. I guess you're a big deal if NASA sends you texts. Maybe I should be a little more, um, interested in your work. What exactly do you do for the government, Gabe?"

He chuckled. "NASA can text you, too, Skye. Nothing to do with my work. Actually, I'm just a star gazing nerd. You'll see."

"Star gazing? Well, that's interesting."

****

An hour later Gabe had dragged two Adirondack chairs out on to the beach and had uncorked a bottle of wine to take with them to the lookout he had created beyond the deck of Mermaid Cottage.

Skye sat on the chair next to him, a goblet of red wine in hand, her eyes upturned to the heavens. "Am I looking for something in particular?"

"Yes. Look toward the northeast." He glanced at his glowing digital watch. "In a minute or so."

The incandescent orb appeared, unmistakably brighter than any surrounding stars, arcing a sweeping, glowing tail like a celestial jet contrail.

She jumped to her feet pointing directly at the phenomenon. "Oh my gosh, Gabe. It's beautiful! What *is* that?"

Gabe stood and joined her, wrapping his arm around her and squeezing her close to his side. "That, love, is the International Space Station."

Chapter 16

A half hour before dawn, Skye tiptoed down the stairs and stopped at the kitchen counter to fill her insulated cup with Kay's strong coffee. She needed a healthy jolt of caffeine to jumpstart her foggy brain after more Gabe-inspired tossing, turning, and sleeplessness. His gentle, almost brotherly peck on her lips last night when he had dropped her off after dinner and stargazing left her yearning and frustrated as never before. He would leave for Washington today. He had promised to call. That was encouraging, at least.

Maybe a little distance would help her get her emotions in check, but she doubted it. She already missed him, and her stomach was in knots worrying that her hot and cold behavior had him believing that she didn't want him. *Nothing* was further from the truth.

On autopilot, she left the house and drove the short distance to the empty beach access parking lot. She left her car as the charcoal sky started to lighten maroon and yellow fringing the distant seascape. She stood on the cutaway through the dune and took a deep breath. The sun began cresting the horizon, a pink neon ball promising a sunny day ahead. This was her favorite time of the day, alone with the majestic sky and ocean. Headlights illuminated the sand in front of her interrupting her solitude. Turning around, she squinted into the glare identifying her friend, Tim, parking his

Jeep next to hers and bounding out of the driver's seat.

"Hey, Skye." He strode across the lot and unlocked the shed housing the ATVs. "I woke up feeling lucky today. I think this is the morning of the first nest."

Always the gentleman, he backed Skye's ATV out first.

She swung her leg over the saddle and sat waiting for him. The idling engine rumbled beneath her as he pulled up next to her. "Fingers crossed. We're long overdue down here. It's not fair the 4X4 has all the nests."

"Damn straight."

Skye tailed Tim's vehicle until they reached the shoreline. She gave him a wave as she headed south, and he turned north. "Good luck."

Maneuvering around galling holes dug in the sand that visitors *should* have filled in before they left the beach yesterday, she swept her gaze perpendicular to the shoreline searching for telltale tracks and at the same time thinking, *Gabe, Gabe, Gabe.*

With her intense beach scanning, she couldn't miss the rapid approach of a jogger from the distance. The shadowy form was too looming to be female. *Gabe!*

Skye wagged her head shaking away the thought. Would she imagine him in every man that she encountered? Focusing on the dunes to her far right, she searched for turtle tracks and ignored the jogger.

"What a beautiful way to start the day," came a hearty baritone she'd recognize anywhere.

She braked and lurched to a stop. Gabe had materialized in front of her. Shirtless, sweaty, and fantasy-handsome, he stood on the sand grinning at her. His smile alone made her weak-kneed.

Skye beamed at him. "I thought you'd be on the road by now. Did you change your plans?"

Her gaze traveled the length of him from defined, ridged muscles on his torso, snug running shorts hugging his narrow waist, down to powerful thigh muscles covered with sable hair. *My God, he is gorgeous.*

"One look at the sky this morning and I had to get in a run before I left. Now, I have another reason to be glad I'm still here." He put his hands on the ATV's handlebars and lowered his head slowly toward her.

The move magnetized her, and she met his lips eagerly, determined to convey that she wanted much more than brotherly kisses like last night. He got the message. She withdrew gently on a sigh.

"Now I'm doubly glad I'm here."

"Me, too." Skye planted her feet in the sand, stood straddling the ATV, wrapped her arms around his neck, and tugged him into another kiss. Female power surged through her. She deepened the kiss swimming in the electrifying tornado of desire he churned in her.

This time Gabe pulled away first. "Lady, you make it very hard to leave. You have no idea what you do to me."

"I think I might. I wish you could stay."

And I'll tell you my truths to explain all. I'm a virgin and the primary heir of the powers of the legend in my generation, each tightly interconnected. The thought of confiding either truth terrified her.

Unlike Bree and Summer, Skye hadn't chosen to follow through with sexual attractions to boys and men she had dated, even though her sisters safeguarded the secret of the legend, too. Maybe Skye had turned her back on intimacy because her power was foremost and not as limited as the other two triplets. Skye had shouldered the most responsibility in keeping family secrets. She took that just as seriously as Aunt Karol always had.

An urgent song calling out an SOS meant solely for her sounded sharply. Skye snapped to attention.

She plopped back down astride the ATV. "I have to go." She waved her arm back and forth in front of her. "Hurry, Gabe. Please move aside."

He immediately sidestepped frowning. "What? Why?"

She yanked her phone out of her back pocket and held it out to him. "Here. Please call Ocean Rescue from my contacts list. Ask for Ray. Tell him there's a surfer with a head injury."

Gabe looked around, a blank expression on his face. "Surfer? Where? What are you talking about?"

"Please help, Gabe. I don't have time to explain. Tell Ray to get to the beach north of Sea Gull Lane." Skye gunned the motor. "I'll meet him there."

She sped along the shoreline thankful that no one was out in front of her, and she could keep her eyes seaward beyond the mammoth breakers.

"I'm coming," she whispered in the wind. "Hold on."

The dolphins swimming close to the shore indicated the path she needed to take, and Skye followed, halting when they did. She flew off the ATV, sloshed into the sea foam until out far enough to dive into an over-arching wave. A bystander might have seen a slim, fair-skinned redhead in shorts and a N.E.S.T. T-shirt enter the pounding waves but wouldn't catch a glimpse of her again until she surfaced far offshore riding mountainous swells. Perhaps the beachcomber might have glimpsed a copper-colored dolphin streaking toward the horizon on the redhead's trajectory—or rather, chalk the sudden disappearance of a woman and appearance of sea creature up to sun blindness.

Skye arrived at the ring of dolphins surrounding a barely conscious teenaged boy. He hung over a surfboard with a bleeding gash on his head. She clasped the edge of the board with both her hands and gripped the sides, white knuckled in the undulating water.

"You did a great job getting him out of the water, Spike." Skye acknowledged the largest dolphin at the foot of the board.

Spike's mate swam close circles around Skye and the injured kid. "Thank you for calling me, Minnie."

Skye awkwardly stripped off her sopping shirt maintaining contact with the surfboard hand by hand, thankful that she wore a sports bra underneath. She balled the shirt up and pressed it against the cut on his forehead.

He groaned.

"That's a good sign," she muttered. "Hey, buddy. You had an accident. Your board conked you on the head. I'm getting you help. Just hang in there."

"Uh..." He raised his head and trained groggy eyes on her. "You a...mermaid?"

"Close enough, kid." She chuckled. "Don't talk. Just lie still. I called for help, and we'll get you to the shore."

His head sagged back down onto the board.

She gazed toward the beach. No sign of the Ocean

Rescue team yet.

The T-shirt that she compressed against his head turned pink beneath her hand.

Like a surging engine, the glinting water swelled and rolled around her, up, down into deep troughs. Bobbing furiously, she struggled to maintain her one-handed grip on the board while applying pressure to his wound.

Please, Sacred Source. I can't do this on my own. Her legs burned and numbed as she continued to vigorously tread water.

"Yes," she said responding to the suggestion that Minnie conveyed.

She flattened both palms on the board's bobbing surface and wove a touch of spellbinding to jettison her body out of the sea to sit straddling the board. Skye leaned forward gripping the board on either side of the boy's sagging body. The pod surrounded her and nudged the surfboard toward land.

Dead ahead of her heaving perch, the Ocean Rescue truck blazed through the beach access and ground to a halt on the sand. Ray and three lifeguards clad in neon orange trunks piled out of the truck, raced toward the shoreline, and thrashed into the sea holding their red rescue boards overhead with one arm. The pod broke up and disappeared underwater as the powerful swimmers approached.

"Thank you," she whispered.

One fin surfaced inches away from Skye's dangling right foot and then disappeared.

Ray and the team must have reached her in minutes, but it felt like hours to Skye. The lifeguards secured the board, and she slipped into the water. She swam and rode the rollercoaster waves body surfing behind Ray's team. Relief swept through her as she gained footing in the sand near the water's edge.

"Great job, Skye. Sorry if we took too long. I got here as fast as I could round up the team." Ray offered a handhold as Skye stumbled in the soft sand.

She regained her balance and then released Ray's hand. "Thanks. I was lucky to be in the right place at the right time. I hope he'll be okay."

"He's one lucky dude that you were on turtle patrol today."

The EMS team emerged on a run over the dunes carrying a stretcher, Gabe in tow. Her heart swelled watching him help the paramedics navigate the deep sand back to the ambulance once they had the boy safely secured on the stretcher.

Door slams sounded and then Gabe reappeared over the dunes racing back to her.

She stood rooted to the spot shaking with adrenaline.

"Oh my God, are you all right?"

Strong arms enveloped her. She nodded her head against the warm bare skin of his shoulder, her teeth chattering.

He held her at arm's length briskly rubbing up and down the sides of her arms.

The breeze from the north fanning her bare skin and sopping clothes had her shivering uncontrollably.

"Let me get you a blanket from the Ocean Rescue truck before they leave." He made to move away, but she circled her arms around his waist and held on tight.

"Just hold me." Tears welled.

What if she hadn't heeded the voices that only she

could hear while chatting with Gabe earlier? What if she hadn't stemmed the surfer's blood flow sufficiently? What if she hadn't done enough to save him? Should she have changed and flown him out of the water legends and secrets be damned? Would a pelican be strong enough to carry his weight? She had nothing to fear from the sea *if* she inhabited a marine body. Should she have stayed in that form? How could she have brought him toward shore in a marine body? As it stood, the sea could have taken her as rapidly as the injured teen.

"You were incredible," Gabe whispered softly, his breath warm on the part of her hair. His powerful arms held her securely against his chest.

"Skye!"

She lifted her head in the direction of the man's voice.

Ray bounded toward them. He handed Skye a T-shirt which she gratefully donned over her wet sports bra. Looking down at her chest, she registered the honor Ray had bestowed on her. "Ocean Rescue? I thought only your elite group could wear one of these."

"You earned it."

"Thanks. This means a lot. How's he doing?"

"He's starting to come to. The paramedics think he has a concussion. He's talking some gibberish though. Nonsense about a red dolphin changing into a beautiful woman and mermaids and such. Gotta run. Thank you both for your help today."

Ray shook Gabe's hand and then headed toward his truck.

"Well, I don't know about a red dolphin, but I certainly know who the beautiful woman is." Gabe tipped a finger under Skye's chin angling her head upward.

"This might not be the right thing to say in this situation, but the way you rushed off to save a life? It was really hot."

Skye burst out laughing.

Gabe put his hand over his heart. "Really."

"Before I forget." He handed Skye her cellphone. "You have a few text messages. I didn't want to invade your privacy, but it kept alerting and the names Bree and Summer kept displaying."

He watched Skye closely as she checked the message icon and opened the app scanning the texts. She had missed six messages each from Bree and Summer.

Of course, her sisters knew she was involved in a dangerous situation. But, of course, they already knew she was okay. She glanced up meeting his eyes. She had no difficulty reading the question swimming in their cocoa-colored depths. *How did they know?*

She held the phone casually in hand. "It's a triplet thing since my earliest memory. If one of us fell on the playground, the other two would know immediately, sometimes actually feeling the pain in our own knee or elbow. You can't imagine how hard it was for me when Summer was at college. Oh, the hangovers!"

Gabe's easy laugh had Skye laughing, too. "I'll text them when I get back to the inn," she said.

"I better go shower and get on the road to Washington."

"I'm so sorry I've made you late."

"Are you kidding?" He clasped her hands and kissed each of her knuckles in turn setting her nerve endings sparking and her heart racing. "You make it impossible to leave."

"I don't want you to leave, either. But you have important meetings, and I have paintings I need to finish for my next show. Now that you have the cottage, maybe you'll come more often."

"My grandfather was very generous with his friends and let them use the cottage all the time. A few have already contacted me to make sure they could still come this summer. How could I say no? But I promise I'll be back as much as I can. We'll figure it out…if you want to…"

"I'll be here waiting." She stood on tiptoe and kissed him with passion hoping he'd get the message of just how much she wanted to figure it out with him.

He moaned drawing her into a tight hug. "You are a witch, and you have me under your spell."

Not technically. We three never resort to changing hearts. She slipped out of his embrace. "I have to bring the ATV back to the shed."

She swung her leg over the saddle and started the motor.

"I'll call you tonight."

"Good. Safe trip." Skye took off down the beach.

"Miss you already," he called out.

She raised her hand over her head and waved. "Miss you too," she whispered.

Chapter 17

Skye had barely opened her gritty eyes when her phone danced buzzing and vibrating on her nightstand. She picked it up and glanced at the Caller ID, "Bree".

As she accepted the call, a Call Waiting popped up. "Summer is on the other line, Bree."

"Patch her in, Skye." Bree's tone left no room to question or object.

Skye tapped where necessary to connect the conference call. "Good morning…"

"You have got to stop!" Bree interjected.

"Yes, you do, please! We're so worried about you. You'll never get a good night's sleep again if you keep this up," Summer boomed in her ear.

"I'm fine. Really," Skye said lamely, not even remotely convincing herself.

She hadn't had a decent night's sleep in weeks. Maybe if she tried blanking her mind entirely, she'd block her sisters out enough to get a grip on her own. At least her sleeplessness last night had nothing to do with Gabe. She lost count of how many ways she and her teenage charge yesterday had drowned in her nightmares.

"Are you *kidding?*" Summer huffed. "You call those nightmares we had all night fine?"

Of course, Summer had the same dreamscape as I did last night. Skye sat up in bed, straightened her spine, and leaned back against the headboard. "I guess it was pretty bad, both in reality and in my dreams. At least in reality we didn't drown."

"Sweetie, you were very brave *and* very smart. Stop second guessing yourself," Bree said.

"Yeah," Summer agreed. "You, above all, should have confidence. You always know how best to bind with the Sacred Source. Not like us lowly earthlings."

Skye hooted a laugh at the long-standing tease between the three of them. In her defense, Skye had never once suggested that either of her sisters was anything less than her equal. They had dubbed themselves earthlings. And Skye? Since childhood Bree and Summer firmly believed her powers had no limit and referred to her as their demigoddess—not altogether sarcastically. "I could have used you lowly earthlings with me yesterday. There are so many ways I might have…lost."

"Well, you didn't. We love you, sweetie, and we wish we were there yesterday, too," Bree said.

The latch clicked riveting Skye's attention on the inward swinging bedroom door.

"So, we're here today," Summer declared as her sisters bounded into the room.

Nothing could have delighted Skye more than Bree and Summer surrounding her with open arms. Possibly, except for Gabe doing the same thing. They didn't give her a chance to get to her feet and hugged her fiercely from each side. Then they plopped down on the foot of her bed wearing identical Cheshire cat grins.

Skye put the phone aside on the night table and wagged her head back and forth in disbelief, alternately gazing into Bree's and Summer's identical pine green eyes, mirror images of her own. If Summer hadn't chopped her hair into Joan-Jett-like punky spikes last year, very few people could have told them apart. Of course, rascally triplets that they were growing up, they loved fooling others by assuming each other's identities. Bree's husband, Jack, and Summer's fiancé, Vinnie, had never had any difficulty telling the three of them apart. Skye wondered how Gabe would fare if they played the game on him.

"He'd know you anywhere, sweetie." Bree said sweetly.

"Wow, I'm impressed," Skye said with conviction. "You're *really* getting good at that."

"Thanks. I'm not sure why, but lately I believe that I might have more Mom in me than I thought."

"So…" Summer wriggled in her seat. "Tell us all the latest with mister Gabriel Hartley."

"Mom looked for me," Skye said.

"She *did*?" Bree sat up straighter on the bed and grabbed Skye's hand. "Well, don't keep us in suspense. What did she see?"

"Only good."

Summer and Bree exchanged knowing glances.

"Well, then, nothing to stop you now. Go for it," Summer said.

"I don't know." Skye wanted to believe that nothing stood in the way of loving him. But realistically? "I'm…in love with him. But I don't think I'll ever find the courage to tell him about the legend. I haven't even told him yet that I'm a virgin. I think I'm hopeless."

"Oh, bull," Summer said. "I was petrified that Vinnie would find out, and I thought I did a great job of hiding it from him all along. And then he watched us change back from dolphin bodies on the beach. He thought it was the coolest thing he ever saw."

"I guess. But what about Jack?" Skye turned her gaze to Bree's face.

"True, Jack was a problem at first. After he saw you and I turning into pelicans in front of his eyes."

"You think?" said Skye.

Bree snorted a laugh. "But the thing is—Jack is my one and only. If Gabe is meant to be yours, nothing between here and the realm of the Sacred Source will change that. Have faith."

Skye absorbed the sweet sentiment. "Thank you." She nodded her head acknowledging her shifting viewpoint. "I needed that."

"Hey, what are sisters for?" Summer beamed at her. "We're here whenever you need us."

"Is that why you both came all this way?" Skye threw off the bedcovers and swung her legs over the side of the bed. "To inject me with a little faith that I can trust my one and only?"

Summer rose to her feet. "There's that. But the real reason we're here is to help with your organizing meeting today."

"*Really?* Oh, that's wonderful." Skye stood up and did a little dance. "I could really use your help. I'm a wreck thinking about public speaking, but I have a lot of important information I want to share, and together we'll do a much better job than I could ever manage alone."

"I don't know about that," Bree said. "But we're determined to help any way we can."

"The meeting's at the community center in two hours. Have you had breakfast?"

"Nope." Summer got to her feet. "We'll go raid Mom's buffet while you get ready. See you downstairs."

****

The triplets approached the newish Community Center, a squat building that looked like a graceless block of mud-colored concrete with strip malls on either side. *Hazel would hate this building.*

"Hazel would hate this building," Summer and Bree echoed Skye's thoughts in unison.

Their adopted ancestor who had built their family home, the classically beautiful Inn of the Three Butterflies, generations ago, had a flair for design.

"In fairness, the back wall is mostly glass that provides a lovely view of the Sound. Hazel might forgive the lack of curb appeal if she could bring herself to go inside."

Skye swung open the door of the Community Center and held it so that Bree and Summer could enter in front of her. She directed her sisters toward the large meeting area that doubled as a gymnasium and sometime Town Hall for Council meetings. The air in the crowded space was stuffy and overwarm from milling bodies. Folding chairs in close arrangement pinched seats a little too close together for comfort.

Bonney waved at Skye from her position at the table that faced the audience in the front of the room.

She turned to Bree and Summer. "I have to sit up there with Bonney and the other coalition representatives. Is that all right?"

Bree touched Skye's arm. "Of course."

Summer waved a hand shooing Skye forward. "We'll find seats; don't worry."

170

Minutes after Skye took her place, Bonney rose from the seat next to her and walked to the microphone stand in front of the table. "Can everybody take a seat, please?" She paused until the ensuing ruckus stopped.

"Good morning. We all know why we're here. We need a solid strategy to meet with the President's administration fact-finding committee, tentatively scheduled in three weeks. We *have* to convince them to reverse the decision to proceed with seismic testing off our shores."

The statement drew thundering applause. Bonney's somber, all-business expression didn't change despite the affirmation from the gathering. "Representing N.E.S.T., the network for endangered sea turtles, and the community of Nags Head at large, let me introduce, Skye Layton. She has the facts you need to hear."

Skye's stomach dropped and stage fright nearly paralyzed her. She sought out a glimpse of her sisters in the crowd. Bree shot her double thumbs up. Summer gestured, peace.

She took Bonney's place at the mic and quiet resolve filled her. "Seismic testing involves blasting the seafloor with air guns which are actually powerful horns. These air guns use loud blasts that go off every ten seconds, twenty-four hours a day, sometimes for weeks. They are so loud that they penetrate through the ocean, miles into the seafloor, and then reflect back to map the location of buried oil and gas deposits. The impact on marine animals and other wildlife is immeasurable. For me, it's unthinkable."

The audience applauded enthusiastically. Skye held up her hand. When the applause died down, she continued, "This process at best disrupts the habitats

171

and feeding of whales, dolphins, sea turtles, and at worst permanently deafens, injures, and even kills."

Hands shot up. Skye pointed to a woman in the front row stretching out her arm dramatically. "Yes ma'am."

"Is this actually happening today?"

Summer spoke out, "May I answer that?"

"Yes," Skye said.

"I had a conversation with your governor yesterday morning. As some of you may know, she was able, because of the public outcry, to impose a ban on the testing when the administration first announced plans to proceed with offshore oil exploration along the Atlantic coast. Her fear is that the ban won't hold, and that the President assembled the fact-finding committee to give the impression that they'll hear out opposing views, but it may be largely symbolic. The governor thinks the President might reverse the ban and proceed anyway."

"Can they do that?" came an indignant male voice.

"Not if we can help it," Skye piped up. "You have no idea how awful and literally unbearable this is to sea turtles, dolphins, and whales. It's the *most* painful, unremitting torture from which there is no escape. Boats pull these air gun rigs along, casting a wide wake of blasting that pursues aggressively. It's impossible to stand."

Bree cleared her throat loudly.

Skye picked up on the cue realizing that she sounded as if she could personally experience the impact of seismic testing. She dared not convey that she *could* offer a personal perspective.

"What I mean is," she regrouped, "this is impossible, and we're not going to stand for it. Thank

172

you."

The assembly applauded Skye to her seat. Bonney replaced Skye at the microphone. "So. Today we need a show of hands. How many of you are interested in going with us to have your voices heard in Raleigh at the committee meeting?"

It seemed to Skye that every hand shot up, including her sisters'. Bonney started to count and changed her mind saying, "Heck, there's a sign-up sheet at the table in back. Please leave your name and text message info on the form. We'll get back to you with timing, meeting place, transportation to Raleigh, and all that.

"Now I'm looking for volunteers. We need to arrange transportation and negotiate costs. We don't have much of a budget as a coalition per se, but we do have interested marine conservation organizations represented here. Maybe someone could organize the representatives and find out if we have any help with paying for the group trip?"

Summer and Bree raised their hands. Bonney called, "Bree?"

"We'll help Skye, and we'll coordinate everything with you."

Bonney gave a decisive head nod. "Sounds like a plan. Any further questions?... No? Then, meeting adjourned. Don't forget to sign that sheet in the back so we know how many coaches to reserve. Thank you all. We'll win this fight."

Chapter 18

Skye tucked her silk, polka-dotted blouse into high-waisted ivory slacks and slipped on tan Manolo Blahnik heels. Checking her outfit in the full-length mirror hanging on the back of her bathroom door, she expertly twisted her hair into a sleek bun on the top of her head.

"You make that look so easy." Kay leaned against the bedroom door frame gazing at Skye.

"When you fix your hair, you make it look even easier. I still can't master the French braids you can do with your eyes closed." Skye switched off the bathroom light, ambled across the room, and packed her hairbrush in the overnight bag spread open on her bed.

"You look beautiful. Is that a new blouse? I love the brown polka dots; and the shoes really pull the style together. It looks like something Summer might wear."

"Busted." Skye laughed. "Summer left the outfit on my bed last night after I told her I was meeting Gabe's mother. I think she was afraid I would wear one of my maxi skirts and flip flops. Which reminds me…" Skye added a skirt and top to the stuffed overnight bag.

"I can't tell you how great it was to have Bree and Summer with me at the meeting yesterday. Especially Summer. You should see her in action, Mom. She's amazing. I wish I had half of her guts. Now that I'll have my sisters by my side, I feel more confident that I can lead the coalition meeting in Raleigh."

"No one has your passion for the ocean or your compassion for the beautiful creatures who live there. You don't need to rely on your sisters. You could do this on your own. But I'm happy that Bree and Summer have joined you to help. You girls are unbeatable when you're together."

Skye tugged the zipper closed on the bulging duffel bag and plopped it on the floor next to the bed with a thud. She paced back into the bathroom to check her makeup one last time.

Skye reemerged into the bedroom.

Kay narrowed her eyes. "You seem nervous. Are you okay?"

"I don't know. When Gabe called and invited me to dinner at his farm, it seemed like a perfect idea. I'm going to be in Norfolk anyway, and it's a short drive over the bay bridge tunnel. Now I'm not so sure I'm ready to meet his mother."

"Why? Do you question your feelings for him?"

"No. It's not that. I'm worried his mother won't like me."

Kay gazed pensively at Skye. "I could say that's ridiculous; of course, she'll like you. You're perfect. But hearing that from your mother doesn't help, does it?"

Skye shook her head.

"How about I say, if she doesn't like you that's her loss? And poor judgment."

"I think Gabe might be the one for me, Mom." Unexpected tears stung her eyes.

"Oh, honey, that's not something to cry about. Finding love is pure joy. Don't worry, go to dinner and just be yourself. How could she not love you? You *are* perfect, you know. Everybody around here thinks that, not just me."

"I love you, Mom." Skye hugged Kay. "I feel bad leaving when Bree and Summer just got here."

"They're sleeping in and will both head home tomorrow. But how exciting that they'll be back soon for the trip to Raleigh. I'm hoping that maybe they'll stay a little longer then."

"Me, too." Skye heaved the satchel up off the floor. "I better get going. Dad probably has the van loaded already."

Kay rose from her seat on the edge of the bed and enveloped Skye in a warm hug. "Have a good time. Just be yourself."

****

Skye helped Mike and the driver finish loading her paintings into the Harrington Gallery's van, kissed her dad on the cheek, hopped into her Jeep, and then tailed the van for the two-hour drive to downtown Norfolk. The gallery was located on Waterside Drive parallel to the Elizabeth River. Skye found a parking space behind the loading zone in front of Harrington Gallery. She slipped out of the driver's seat, stretched her back, and inhaled the wet loamy scent of the river.

Scott Harrington hurried around the reception desk as Skye walked through the gallery's front door.

He gave her a hug. "It is *so* good to see you, Skye. Sit. Sit."

Scott led Skye toward the teal S-shaped sectional. "Tell me all about your trip to Palm Springs. I heard through the grapevine you had very successful showings."

"I did. Thanks to my aunt."

"You're way too modest. Your paintings are amazing. I can't wait to hang your latest work. The photos you sent are divine. Did Marcus tell you that we've sold three of the paintings just from the pamphlet? The new horse series is magnificent."

"I painted a few for the Corolla Wild Horse Fund's auction and was just inspired to keep going."

Marcus, Scott's partner in business and in life, strutted into the room toting a bottle of wine in an ice bucket in the crook of his arm and three glasses held by the stems in one hand. Towering over Scott, he bussed a kiss on the top of his head. After he set down the wine and goblets on the glass table next to the sofa, he planted a kiss on Skye's cheek.

"My God, Bella," Marcus said. "The paintings are even better in person. Scott and I are in love with the horses. There was one painting that wasn't pictured in the advance photos you sent. It's labelled Corolla Wild Horse Fund."

"Oh right. I'm sorry. We shouldn't have loaded that one on your van."

"I figured. I'm having them rewrap it and stowed in the back of your car. Now..." Marcus filled a glass and handed it to Skye. "We must celebrate."

"No wine for me, Marcus. I have to drive." Skye offered the goblet back.

He waved his hand in dismissal. "Just a sip, darling. You can't leave until we toast to your success." Marcus filled the other two glasses.

Scott and Marcus raised their glasses prompting her to follow suit.

"Here's to another sellout showing," Marcus said.

"And I'd like to propose a toast to my future

husband," Scott chimed in.

"*What?*" Skye said jumping to her feet.

Marcus blushed extending his left hand toward Skye, his palm down, fingers spread. "Scott proposed last night. And of course, I said yes!"

Skye took hold of his hand admiring the white gold band circled by black diamonds on his ring finger. "It's beautiful. I'm so happy for both of you."

She gave each of them a hearty hug.

"Come into the back room," Scott said. "I have lunch on the table. We can talk about our wedding plans, and then we should be ready to view your paintings."

Her salad was delicious, and Skye had fun listening to Scott's and Marcus's excitement about their marriage arrangements. After a few tweaks with lighting and rearranging a few of the paintings, Skye was pleased with the display of her work. She made a quick trip to the powder room to check her hair and makeup and then said goodbye to the men.

Outside behind the wheel, she sent a text to Gabe that she was on her way and then entered the farm's address in her Maps App.

The route was a straight shot to the bridge tunnel and then a short drive on Route 13 until SIRI instructed her to turn onto a narrow road that wound its way through a wooded area ending in front of ornate white iron gates each topped with two huge letter M's. Skye's heart leaped at the sight of Gabe leaning sexily against the brick column on the left side of the gates.

She lowered her window. "Hey there," she called out.

He sauntered over to the car, leaned in through the

open window, and gave her a slow delicious kiss.

"Wow," she said when she caught her breath. "Do you greet all your guests that way, Mr. Hartley?"

"Only the beautiful, surfer saving, turtle nest hunting artists that drop by."

He ducked his head back out of the window, strode over to the gate, punched in a code on the security pad mounted on the brick column, and then got into her car with her.

The gates slowly swung open. "What do the M's stand for?"

"My grandfather named the ranch after my grandmother, Madelyn, and my mother, Meredith—the two loves of his life."

"That is so romantic."

"I wish you could have met my granddad. He was a gruff man. Only a few of us really knew him. He was a softy when it came to his family. I loved him a lot."

Skye squeezed Gabe's hand and then rolled slowly down the driveway, parking in the circle fronting an imposing white porticoed mansion.

"I'll show you around the grounds and bring your things to the guest house after dinner, if you don't mind. My mom is waiting for us."

Gabe bounded out of the car, rounded the front bumper, and opened Skye's door.

She reached into the backseat and tugged a shopping bag into the front seat.

"What do you have there?"

"Hostess gift for your mother." Her hands visibly trembled.

"What's wrong? Are you okay?"

"I'm fine. But I'm a nervous wreck."

"Oh, you have no reason to worry. Mom is very gracious. And she's bound to see right away what I see. My beautiful lady."

Skye felt only slightly less intimidated with his encouragement.

He took hold of her hand and ushered her into the house. "We're here," Gabe called.

"I'm in the blue room, Gabriel," came the regal tones of his mother's slight southern drawl.

Skye's heels clicked on the marble floor echoing as she walked wherever Gabe led her, which made her even more self-conscious at the racket that she made. His mother would hear her coming like a heavy-footed oaf. They passed through one room after another until they entered a blue one, *the* blue one. Meredith Hartley stood facing the door framed from behind by illumination from floor to ceiling doors overlooking lush green pastures dotted by beautiful specimens of horseflesh.

Skye had the distinct impression that Gabe's mother had staged exactly how she wanted this meeting to unfold from start to finish. The tightly composed expression on her face and slight narrowing of her eyes gazing at Skye spoke volumes. Dressed in a black St. John knit pantsuit, the petite matriarch, without a blonde hair out of place, looked ready to do battle with this female contender for her son's heart.

"Mom, this is Skye Layton," Gabe said.

Meredith extended her right hand. The smile on her face never quite reached her aqua blue eyes. "It is a pleasure to meet you, Skye."

The handshake Skye accepted was cool and brief. "Thank you for inviting me to dinner, Mrs. Hartley.

I've been looking forward to meeting you."

Skye dangled the shopping bag out toward his mother. "This is for you."

"Please call me Meredith." She turned her back and stepped to a cluster of armchairs around a coffee table with a bowl of fruit and a charcuterie platter in the center.

"Gabriel, be a dear and get the drinks." She waved her hand toward a carved oak bar in the corner of the room.

Skye put down the gift bag near Meredith's feet and then took a seat opposite her.

"What's this?"

"A small gift to thank you for your hospitality," Skye said.

Meredith slid the bag nearer and dipped her hand inside, extracting the 5X7 canvas wrapped loosely with tissue paper.

"Oh my," she exclaimed inspecting the tiny painting of a small, white-domed church overlooking the Aegean Sea. "This church looks exactly like the one where we went to Mass on our honeymoon. How could you possibly know?"

"Well, of course, I didn't know that was a church that you discovered on your honeymoon. When I visited my Aunt Karol, I was inspired by some of her paintings. I painted a few landscapes when I returned home. This one seemed meant for you. I hope you like it."

"I'm familiar with your aunt's work. Did you copy one of hers?"

"No, I paint from imagination."

"Well... Thank you for a thoughtful gift."

Meredith lowered her eyes. "You obviously have a lot of imagination," she muttered.

Was that a compliment or an insult? Skye eagerly took a gulp out of the glass of wine that Gabe handed to her and then nibbled on a cracker to offset the alcohol. She absolutely needed her wits about her around Gabe's mother.

A woman appeared in the doorway and announced that dinner was served in dulcet tones. Heaven help the person who raised their voice in this house, Skye thought.

They have servants? What else didn't she know about Gabe?

Gabe and Skye followed Meredith into the dining room where candlelight gleamed on the mirror finish of the sprawling mahogany table. Gabe pulled out the chair at the head of the table for his mother. He seated Skye cater-corner from her. The moment Gabe sat down across from Skye, three young women slipped noiselessly into the room and placed salads in front of each of them—crisp lettuce and orange slices with sliced strawberries and a light poppyseed dressing, according to Meredith.

"This is delicious," Skye said after her first bite.

"It's Gabriel's favorite," came the clipped response from the head of the table.

Apparently, it wasn't Meredith's favorite. She picked at the greens and moved food around on the plate instead of actually putting anything in her mouth.

The salad plates were replaced when Meredith rang a little bell.

Really?

The main course was placed in front of Skye. She

gazed askance at the big chunk of filet mignon topped with jumbo shrimp on her plate. Thankfully, the sides of new potatoes and green beans would provide Skye with dinner.

"Mom, you've outdone yourself." Gabe dug into the steak with gusto.

"Only the best for my boy."

"Is there a problem with your dinner?" Meredith's penetrating gaze bore into her.

Gabe turned his attention to Skye's plate.

"Mom, didn't you tell chef that Skye's a vegan?" He rose from his seat shoving his chair away from the table and grabbed the edge of Skye's plate in hand.

"Sit down, Gabriel. I'll ring for a girl."

The tone of Meredith's voice registered as a slap in the face to Skye.

Gabe ignored the command lifting Skye's plate off the table. "I'll be right back."

"I'm sorry for the bother, Meredith," Skye said to fill the vacuum when Gabe left the room.

"Yes, well. I forgot Gabe mentioned you're one of those bleeding hearts people."

Slap.

"I doubt he phrased it that way," Skye said carefully. "It's a personal choice I made a long time ago."

"Seems to me your health might suffer with such an imbalanced diet," she huffed.

Slap number two.

Skye sat close-mouthed avoiding argument and literally counted the seconds until Gabe reappeared with a plate heaped with vegetables in hand.

He winked as he placed her meal in front of Skye.

"Thank you."

"Of course."

Meredith sighed. She cut a big piece of steak, popped the whole thing in her mouth, and laboriously chewed.

Gabe spurred dinner conversation bringing up agreeable topics, but Meredith seemed intent on contrariness.

The Inn—"Oh, your parents are hotel workers."

Slap.

Her career—"It's interesting trying to make a living painting pictures."

Slap.

Her studio—"You still live with your parents?"

Slap again.

Gabe tried valiantly and diplomatically to defend her, regroup, and find something his mother wouldn't slap down in one way or another.

When the dessert dishes were cleared Meredith rose from her seat and excused herself.

For a few minutes Skye enjoyed silence and blessed relief from sniping.

Gabe raised his eyebrows rounding his eyes. "That went well."

Skye burst into tears.

Chapter 19

Seeing her cry ripped a hole in Gabe's heart. He rushed around the table, napkin in hand, and dabbed away the streaks on her cheeks. She rose slowly to her feet, and he wrapped her in his arms.

"I'm sorry," she murmured, her breath warm against his shoulder. "I don't know why I'm crying."

He squeezed her tighter aching that his mother had treated this soft woman so coldly. "You have no reason to apologize. I apologize for Mother. I don't know what that was all about, but I won't accept that behavior toward you from her or anybody."

She raised her head and cast a stricken gaze at Gabe. "Please don't. I can't stand the thought of causing problems with your family. I just wanted her to like me."

Her chest heaved as she took a deep breath, a soft pressure against his torso. Despite the tension at dinner, all Gabe wanted was this, now: to have her here, in his arms.

"The strange thing is, I'm sure she likes you. How could she not? You're perfect."

Skye burst out laughing. "Yeah, well, notify your mom that she truly likes perfect me."

Gabe clasped her soft, small hand. "Let's get out of here. A few of my friends are meeting at a bar tonight. Want to join them?"

Skye wrinkled her nose. "I don't know... I think

I've had enough of introductions for one night."

Gabe was determined to bring shy, sweet Skye into his world, step by tiny step. "These are good people," he assured her. "I promise you'll have fun. Trust me; you'll really like them all."

"I'm more worried about them liking me at this point. But okay. I trust you."

"Let's drop your things at the guest house, and we'll head out."

Gabe drove Skye's Jeep past the stables and pulled up in front of the guest house, a single story, wood frame bungalow painted white. He parked, handed Skye the keys, got out of the car, and headed to the passenger side to hold open the door for her.

"It's nothing fancy, but I think you'll be comfortable." He pointed to his house next door. "That's my place."

"Your farm is amazing." She followed Gabe to the back of the car gazing around her. "It's so beautiful— the horses, the pastures, the stables, and the rolling green hills. I feel a painting coming on."

He grinned. "I'll buy it."

She hooted a laugh and opened the hatch of the jeep.

"What's this?" Gabe indicated a wrapped frame next to a satchel.

"Oh. It's a painting that got mixed up with the delivery to the gallery."

"I'll buy it," Gabe said reaching for the painting.

Skye widened her sparkling green eyes. "That's crazy. You don't even know what it is."

"I don't care. You painted it, therefore, I bet it's amazing."

She snorted and shoved the painting farther back into the cargo space. "You sound just like my dad."

"Name your price." He leaned into the trunk and grabbed an edge of the frame.

Skye chuckled as she lightly swatted his hand away. "I'll think about it. Now let me get changed so we can go get a nice strong drink."

"You look wonderful tonight." Gabe reached for Skye's hand as he drove his sedan through the open gate.

"Thank you. You look pretty good yourself."

Like her, Gabe wore jeans and had tucked in a snowy white dress shirt. Skye had chosen a white cashmere cropped sweater—a matched pair.

"Tell me again who I'm going to meet tonight."

"My friends from school. We've known each other for years."

"Okay. Hopefully they'll be more...accepting than your mother."

"I really am sorry that she hurt your feelings. In her defense she has been having a really hard time since my grandfather died. I try to cut her some slack."

"I understand. I'll do the same. But after that, shall we say, tense dinner, I'm so ready to have some fun. A tequila sunrise would sure hit the spot right about now."

After a ten-minute drive, Gabe pulled the car into a packed parking lot off Route 13. He, as always, held open the door for her, clasped her hand, and strolled across the cracked macadam into the crowded bar. Still holding her hand, he wound his way through the tables until he halted at a table for eight, occupied by three beaming couples.

"Finally!" A burly man shot up from his seat and

slapped Gabe on the back. "I told them you would make it. We signed you up."

"Sorry we're running late. Everyone, I want you to meet Skye," Gabe said.

A chorus of hellos sounded.

One of the women patted the chair next to her. "Come sit here, Skye. I'm Mavis." She pointed to the backslapper. "And that's my husband Mike."

Skye slipped into the seat next to Mavis. "Nice to meet you both."

"We're the loudest of the group," Mavis continued, gesturing to her left. "This is Theresa and Sascha. They're the calmest, and finally this is Kathy and Paul. They're the oldest."

"Oh! Very funny," Kathy said. "I'm one month older than you."

"Well, that makes you the oldest, now, doesn't it?" Mavis barked a contagious laugh.

Skye joined in, instantly liking these people as Gabe had predicted. Before she could accept the glass of beer that Sasha offered her, Gabe set a tall tequila sunrise in front of her.

"Bless you," she teased. "Mike, what did you mean when you said you signed Gabe up?" Skye savored a long sip of her drink.

"It's couples karaoke night," Mavis chimed in. "We've been singing duets for over a year, and this the first time Gabe brought someone, so now he has to enter the contest, too."

"Yeah. Instead of just critiquing all of us," Mike added.

I'm the first Gabe ever brought to hang out here with his friends? She couldn't resist. "You never brought Sharon?" she murmured in his ear.

Amusement danced in his coal-brown eyes. "Nope."

"So now I have to sing for my tequila sunrise?" Skye addressed the group.

Gabe wrapped an arm around her back as if shielding her. "Don't feel any pressure. We don't have to sing if you don't want to."

"It sounds like fun." Skye picked up the pitcher of beer from the middle of the table and passed it to Mavis. "Drink up, everybody. The more you drink, the better I'll sound."

The laughter and din of conversation increased proportionally with the number of drinks served. Kathy passed Skye the list of available karaoke songs. Gabe dipped his head close to hers scrutinizing the choices, his nearness pure pleasure.

"Fair warning. I don't sing," Gabe said. "Maybe in the shower where I sound damn good," he joked, "but never in public."

"The last time I sang in a bar was in Cambridge when Summer was in college."

"Karaoke?"

"Let's just say it was too many tequila sunrises."

Gabe grinned and squeezed her shoulder.

They decided on a duet by Calum Scott and Leona Lewis. The competition started when the first couple stepped onto a small stage in the corner of the bar. They were pretty good, awarded a smattering of applause when they finished. Mavis and Mike did a great job with *You're The One That I Want* from Grease.

Mammoth butterflies fluttered in Skye's stomach as Gabe led her by the hand to the stage after several more couples braved the evening's judgment.

"Do you want to sing the Calum or Leona part?" Gabe whispered, making her laugh out loud.

The music started. Gabe sang the first verse, his voice strong and deep. She closed her eyes to block out the audience, concentrating on the lovely melody and lyrics of the second verse, her solo.

Skye opened her eyes as the duet began gazing into Gabe's sparkling eyes. "And swim every ocean," she sang harmonizing with him, "'cos I need you to see that you are the reason."

Half into the final verse, she realized that the audience had fallen silent. The music ended. Gabe enfolded her in his arms and kissed her softly. The crowd erupted in cheers and applause. The emcee declared Gabe and Skye the winners.

A hot blush crept up to her hairline as he led her back to the table. Gabe raised the trophy overhead in triumph.

"Ringer," Paul quipped.

Seated at the table, Skye finished her drink in one gulp.

"My God," Kathy gushed, "you sounded just like Leona Lewis."

"Hey, buddy," Sascha said as he poured Gabe another beer, "if this Senate thing doesn't work out, you two could take it on the road."

Skye truly enjoyed everything about Gabe's friends. They not only welcomed her, but they also made her feel like she had always been a part of the group.

She debated ordering another drink to spend more time there.

It's time. Please bring him home. The plea rang like an alarm in Skye's head. *I need help.*

Skye closed her eyes. The vision of a large, black horse materialized—surely the source of the call for help in her mind. Opening her eyes, she faked a yawn.

"It's getting late," Gabe interpreted her gesture. "I think we'll call it a night."

Mavis stood up in her place and hugged Skye as she rose from her seat. "We have to do this again soon."

Gabe's friends chorused agreement and promised to get in touch soon.

"I would love that," Skye said, meaning it.

Back in Gabe's luxurious car, Skye sank into the leather seat, holding the coveted trophy on her lap.

She closed her eyes and concentrated on relaying that Gabe was on his way, relieved when she sensed the message received.

"That was so much fun. Thank you for a wonderful night." Skye squeezed Gabe's hand.

"Honestly, I should thank you for coming with me. You have an incredible voice. Did you sing in school?"

"No, except for mandatory chorus classes. Normally, the idea of performing for an audience is the last thing I'd ever consider."

"Well, you could have fooled me. You knocked it out of the park."

"We can thank tequila for helping us to win this little baby." She patted the trophy.

Gabe drove down the winding road leading to the farm. The gates hung open. He frowned. "That's odd. Brad never leaves the gates open."

"Who's Brad?"

"Brad Thompson. He ran the place for my

grandfather and has stayed on to help my mother."

Lights blazed in the main stable ahead.

"Huh," Gabe said. "Do you mind if we stop for a minute and check on things in the stable? Something's not right here."

"Not at all." Skye had no doubt that the message she had heard originated from this place.

Brad rushed toward the car. Gabe and Skye hopped out to meet him.

"What's going on?" Gabe said.

"It's Storm. She started acting anxious and restless, then her placental fluids rushed over a half hour ago. I called you and left a message."

"Damn it." Gabe pulled his phone from his pocket and powered it on. "I turned my phone off in the bar. Did you call Dr. Nancy?"

"Yes, she's on the way."

Skye drifted into the stable to Storm's stall. Pain and fear glittered in the mare's beautiful black eyes.

"It's okay. We're here now. You're going to do fine," Skye soothed as she approached Storm and placed her hand gently on the mare's head.

"You shouldn't be so close," Brad said coming up behind Skye.

Skye didn't move, rather she continued to reassure the horse in a hushed voice. She rubbed her hand on the quivering animal's back and then tenderly massaged the side of her belly.

Hey, little man, you're facing the wrong way. Turn yourself around for your mama. That's it, little one, keep turning. Good boy.

Skye felt the colt roll beneath her hand. Satisfied, she stepped back and let Storm take charge. In a few short minutes, the colt's feet emerged followed by his jet-black face, so like his mother's.

Brad's mouth hung open gazing at Skye. "How did you do that?"

"Do what?"

"Turn the foal around like that."

"I didn't turn the foal. I just massaged Storm's belly to calm her down."

Brad scratched his head. "Wait. That's not what…"

A woman rushed into the stable pulling up short outside Storm's stall. "What's up with our girl? Oh, look at that handsome boy. Good job, Storm."

She turned toward Skye and held out her hand. "Hi. I'm Nancy Canovan, the vet around here."

"Nice to meet you, Doctor Canovan. I'm Skye Layton. He's a beauty, isn't he?"

"That he is. Comes from excellent stock." Nancy observed the mini-me colt nestled at his mother's side. "I must have misunderstood your message, Brad. I thought there was a problem."

"Sorry to bother you, Nancy. Storm appeared to be in distress."

"No bother at all. The little guy looks great, Gabe. His breathing is steady, and he's bright and alert. Give them some peace and quiet and in about two hours he should stand and start to nurse. I see you have fresh water ready for him. Good. No need for me to hang around, but if something changes, call or text. Nice to meet you, Skye."

"Same here," Skye said.

The men escorted Nancy to her car leaving Skye alone with mother and son.

Thank you. The soulful eyes fixated on Skye.

"It was my pleasure," Skye whispered.

Gabe returned to the stall alone. He slipped his arm around her waist and joined her in gazing at the peaceful horses. The little colt's head moved left and right surveying his new surroundings. His legs twitched.

"He looks like he's raring to go." Gabe grinned. "I'll walk you to your cottage. I'm going to stay up a while and watch this little guy get his legs."

Chapter 20

"I'd like to stay, too, if you don't mind. I'm way too excited to sleep," Skye said.

"I'd love that."

Gabe's simple statement filled her with pleasure.

He walked her over to the bench near the stable's door. "This might be more comfortable. I'll get us something to drink."

Gabe opened a cabinet door that concealed a small refrigerator, selected a couple bottles of water, and then joined Skye on the bench.

The soft expression in his dark brown eyes thrilled her. There was nowhere she'd rather be than there, now, with him. Despite his mother's cool reception, Skye didn't regret visiting his family home. She vowed to somehow break through her icy exterior and find common ground with Meredith Hartley. After all, Skye loved her son, too.

"This reminds me of the night Ebony Storm was born minus the thunder and lightning," Gabe said draping his arm around Skye's shoulder. "Granddad and I assisted with the labor until the vet arrived. When Storm was born, he said I should name her. I was thirteen and couldn't believe I'd received such a huge honor. The foal had a jet-black coat, and her eyes flared with temperament. Ebony Storm seemed to fit."

"Do you have a name picked out for this little guy?" she asked.

The colt's head turned at the sound of her voice. She knew he sensed a kindred spirit.

"Onyx Thunder. What do you think?"

"I love it. Storm and Thunder; those names are perfect."

Skye nestled her head against his chest feeling utterly at peace. In minutes she surrendered to sleep.

****

Snickers roused Gabe. Pale rays of sunlight haloed her auburn hair. His arm had long since fallen asleep. Worth it.

Gabe leaned to whisper in her ear dipping into the aura of floral perfume that still lingered on her skin. "Good morning, beautiful."

"Um…" She blinked open her eyes and then straightened up on the bench, stretching her arms over her head. "Morning."

"I could get used to waking up next to you." He nuzzled her neck.

Brad appeared in the doorway carrying a sack of feed. "Ahem. Did I…interrupt, er, something?"

Gabe rose from the bench and held out a hand to Skye. "We fell asleep while admiring our newborn there."

"That is one handsome colt." Brad leaned against Storm's stall.

Gabe strolled over to Brad's side. "What do you think of the name Thunder?"

"I like it." Brad picked up the pail in the corner of the stall and walked toward the back of the stable.

"I think I'd like to have a shower and change these clothes before I get on the road," Skye said.

"I need to do the same thing. Are you hungry?"

"Famished."

He chuckled. "Our breakfast buffets around here are legion. Meet you at the main house when you're done with your shower? Say, in an hour?"

"Sure. I'll pack my car and drive there. Okay to park in the circle in front of the house?"

"Of course. Come on. I'll take you to your cottage."

Gabe parked behind Skye's Jeep in front of the guest house, slipped out of the Audi, and hustled around to the passenger side to hold open Skye's door. "Hang on a minute," he said.

He rooted in the back seat for the karaoke trophy. Gabe handed the memento to Skye. "Take this home with you. I'll keep the next one we win."

She accepted the prize and paced over to her car. While she stowed the trophy in the back of the jeep, Gabe noticed the wrapped painting again.

"Name your price," he said laying a hand on the frame.

"You're nuts. You don't even know what it looks like."

"I still want it. I don't care how much you charge for it."

She wagged her head and rolled her eyes. "I don't know what I'm going to do with you, Gabriel. All right, on one condition. Donate whatever you'd like to pay to the Corolla Wild Horse Fund. I earmarked this as a donation for their upcoming fundraiser auction."

"Deal." He slid the painting toward him and lifted it out of the trunk. Holding the canvas's frame in one hand, he cupped her face with his other hand and kissed her gently.

The sugar sweet taste of her lips, after an all-nighter in a barn with no toothpaste in sight, amazed him. He didn't want to let her go even for a brief hour to shower and dress for the day. But they both had full days ahead. No choice.

Gabe ended the kiss rewarded with the dreamy expression she wore on her face. "Mm," she said. "Thank you."

"My pleasure." He couldn't let her go before locking down more future time with her no matter how busy their schedules. "When can I see you next?"

"What do you mean? At breakfast, right?"

"I mean after today."

"Oh." Skye huffed a laugh. "Well, when's the next time you're planning to stay at Mermaid Cottage?"

"That's the thing. It's rented for the next month."

Skye pursed her lips. "Hmm. I guess we have to wait until it's available."

"Could I fly you to D.C. for a long weekend? Next weekend?" he urged, hopeful that she'd dislike a longer separation just as much as he would.

"You are much more the jet setter than I am, Gabe. Maybe you could come stay at the inn next weekend? Meet my parents?"

He jumped at the chance. "Yes. That's a great idea. I'll see you at breakfast."

Gabe carried the painting into his house and propped it against the couch before heading to the shower. Since he had a full agenda of afternoon meetings, he donned a white dress shirt, slate gray slacks, and a red power tie. Leaving his suit jacket in his closet to hang up in his car when he collected his things after breakfast, he went outside to the Audi.

Gabe noticed that Skye's Jeep was no longer parked in front of her cottage.

Inside the main house, Gabe pulled up short to the side of the archway of the dining room to eavesdrop when he heard Skye's and Meredith's voices.

"I hope I did nothing to offend you last evening," Skye said. "If I did, I apologize."

"Perhaps offend isn't the right word," Meredith retorted.

Gabe frowned at his mother's curt tone. Ready to break up what sounded like instigating an argument, he paused hearing Skye's response.

"I never mince words," Skye said.

Gabe pulled back, pleased at Skye's no-nonsense tone.

"I sincerely felt a tension between us, and I don't want that. Family is very important to me. I care deeply about Gabe and, of course, I respect you."

No reason to ride to Skye's rescue, Gabe thought, admiring her calm ability to stand up to the formidable Meredith Hartley.

"*If* you care deeply about my son, you'll see how important it is for him to select exactly the right life partner."

"And what *exactly* qualifies as the right life partner for him in your view?"

"One who understands the intricacies of campaigning and creating the right image for my son's ambitions. His wife will surely be the First Lady one day. I'm sure you can see what I mean before your relationship...gets too serious."

Gabe had had enough. He stalked into the dining room where he encountered Skye already shoving away from the table. Fire flared in her sea green eyes as her gaze met his eyes.

"I'm leaving," she spit out.

"I'll walk you out." He intercepted her before she reached the archway and sheltered her against his side.

Skye turned to face Meredith. "Thank you for dinner," she said, ever courteous. "I'm sorry we got off on the wrong foot. Perhaps that will change."

"Gabriel, I—"

"I'll speak with you in a minute," he cut her off.

Skye trembled beneath his hand striding beside him through the house, out the front door, and down the stairs to the circular driveway.

"I hope you're fighting mad after that tirade and not hurt. Because I sure as hell am fighting mad," he said.

"Honestly, I don't think I've ever been so insulted in my life."

"Yeah. Well, there's no excuse for her treating you that way, and I'll set her straight before I leave."

Skye halted at the driver's door of her car and turned to face him, frowning. "Gabe, she doesn't think I have the necessary pedigree to fit in with your career."

She furrowed her brow deeper. "Your mother's probably right even though it feels like a gigantic snub. I'm not political at all. First Lady? The idea is terrifying. I'm so sorry, Gabe, I should have thought before…"

Tears welled in her eyes.

"Before what, darling?"

"Before I fell…" She bit the corner of lip wagging her head. "Never mind."

Anger at his mother's harshness and her obsession

with his political future pierced him. What kind of future didn't include Skye? He couldn't envision it; didn't want to imagine life without her.

"Skye, I want you. Not some politician's helpmate. Not some image conscious partner like my mother has in mind. You. I don't know what I want to do after my term in the Senate ends. Do I even want to continue in politics? For the record, a presidential run is not my idea. I love my mother, but I make my own decisions. Don't worry, okay?"

She nodded yes, but he wasn't convinced.

"Can I still come visit your family next weekend?"

Skye swiped a hand under her eyes and smiled through her tears. She sniffled. "Do you still want to come? Oh, Gabe…"

Fresh tears streamed down her cheeks. "I don't want to hold you back. I'm in…"

His heart leapt. *She's in love with me.* Gabe clasped both her hands gently. "Don't cry, sweetheart, please. I love you, too."

Her jaw dropped. Huge green eyes sparkling with tears gaped at him. "You *do*? But," she sputtered, "you don't even know me."

He looked at her askance. "Of course, I do. And I'll get to know you a lot better when I meet your family next weekend. Is it still a date?"

Her face brightened. "Yes."

"Good. Then there's nothing left, but this." He swept her into his arms and held her tightly.

She arched her neck and looked up at him, her lips a tantalizing offering he had no intention to refuse. Gabe kissed her deeply, longingly, assured when she kissed him back with equal passion.

He gently let her loose and then opened the car door for her. She slipped into the driver's seat and gazed at him fixedly through the window as he closed the door. Skye lowered the window and crooked her arm on the sill.

Gabe leaned in and pecked her lips. "Safe trip."

"You, too."

Skye put both hands on the wheel.

"One more thing before you go," he said.

She narrowed her eyes and tilted her head.

"I think you'd make an amazing First Lady."

Her burst of laughter was the last thing he heard as the window raised.

He watched her drive away from him already experiencing the hollowness of her absence. She drove through the gates and waved a hand. Once her Jeep was out of sight, Gabe strode back into the house on a bead toward the dining room.

Meredith was still seated at the table when he returned. "Gabriel…"

He held up a hand, stop. "I heard the entire exchange, Mother, starting with Skye's apologizing for somehow offending you. What possessed you to treat her this way?"

She shrugged. "I just presented reality to her, that's all. Your future is bright. Nothing should stand in the way."

"I want to make this clear. Skye has never, would never stand in the way of my work, just like I would never interfere with hers. Just because you and the Party seem to have decided my future, does not mean that I choose the future you have designed. I don't want to fight about this, Mother, but I won't tolerate your treatment of the woman I love."

"The woman...you *love*? Gabriel, be realistic. Do you really see a...bohemian with you in the White House?"

Gabe snorted in derision. "Bohemian? Is that how you see her? Mom, if you'd drop all this ridiculous snobbery and really get to know her, you'd find that she is loving and creative and talented and kind and everything you could ever hope for in a future daughter-in-law. Get used to the idea. Because number one, I don't necessarily see myself in the White House, and number two, I do see myself with Skye. Can you bring yourself to be more civil in the future?"

Meredith heaved her chest.

"For me?" Gabe pressed.

She huffed. "All right. Whatever you wish. I don't want to argue with you, either."

"Good." He bussed her cheek. "I have to get back to Washington. I'll call soon."

"Fine, Gabriel. Please drive carefully."

"Always."

Gabe went back to his house ready to pack and begin the drive to D.C. He grabbed the handle of his duffel in one hand and the wrapped canvas in the other and then had second thoughts. Gabe set his luggage and the artwork back down and then carefully unwrapped the painting.

He stood transfixed by the vivid images before him.

Storm and Thunder stood in the shallows on a beach. He could almost hear the waves breaking and splashing against their legs.

How could she have painted his mare and her foal

in perfect detail before last night? How was this possible?

Chapter 21

Skye couldn't have created a more picture-perfect day with her brushstrokes on canvas. The azure sky dazzled, sun dappled waves rolled hypnotically toward the shore, and the scent of flowers rode on the gentle breeze. She relaxed on the inn's deck with her feet propped up on the railing and basked in her glorious surroundings while sipping lemon tea. She checked the time on her phone—again. Now maybe an hour or so to go before Gabe arrived.

The sliding glass door whooshed open behind her.

Kay sat down in the Adirondack chair next to Skye. She cupped a mug of tea in her hands, took a tiny sip, and then propped her feet up on the railing, too. "I'm so glad we gave the rooms a deep cleaning last week. It was a breeze to organize for the guests today."

"I didn't think we had any reservations until next week."

"Four rooms were reserved on the website on Wednesday. The reservation is only for two nights, so it's a quick turnaround. Dad will barbeque dinner tonight if you want to join us."

"I'm not sure what Gabe has in mind for dinner."

"I'm looking forward to meeting him; so is your dad."

"I hope you like him, Mom."

"Of course, I will." Kay squeezed Skye's knee and rose from her chair. "How could I not? He has excellent taste in women."

Skye laughed. "You are so biased."

"Of course, I am. What mother isn't? Doesn't make me wrong, though."

Kay closed her eyes and tilted her face toward the sun. "What a gorgeous day. Have you planned anything special to do while Gabe is here? By the way, I chose the private cottage for him. I thought he might like that."

Skye thought about the sleeping arrangements when she had visited his farm. "He absolutely will like that. Thanks, Mom. We don't really have anything scheduled while he's here other than spending time with you and Dad. He mentioned that he has been slammed with meetings all week. I thought he might just want to be a beach bum for a couple of days."

"That sounds perfect." Kay squinted and fixated on the back of the building as if she could see through walls. "Your dad is back. I better get in there before he helpfully puts the groceries away and I can't find anything."

Skye followed her mother into the kitchen and helped unpack the groceries. Still left with time to kill, she put together a pot of the Inn's signature BBQ sauce and then set the heat on a low simmer.

Her text chime sounded. Skye's pulse raced reading Gabe's message. He had just crossed the bridge and was on the sandbar. If the traffic cooperated, he should arrive in about a half hour. She wiped her hands on a kitchen towel and headed upstairs to her room to change.

Donning her favorite gypsy skirt, eager anticipation rushed through her. She tied her tangerine T-shirt in a knot at her waist thinking about the mixed bag of emotions that lingered after meeting his mother and visiting his farm. Could she navigate his world *if...*?

She decided not to think about uncertainty. Today was about Gabe in her world. Skye hurried downstairs and outside to the front deck to wait for him.

Skye had just taken a seat when she heard a car's approach. She jumped up, eager to greet Gabe, but instead of his car or truck, a sleek stretch limo turned off the Inlet road and rolled slowly toward the Inn. Hiding her disappointment, she descended the porch stairs to welcome the expected guests.

The back door swung open before the driver reached it. Four roly-poly Boston Terriers plopped out of the car onto the parking apron. Skye squatted down, her hand outstretched, palm up, signaling the dogs to make a beeline toward her, bumping into each other as they came.

"Ladies! Your manners, please!" came a familiar female voice.

As if doused by ice water the four pups skidded to a halt and sat at attention training googly eyes on the car.

Aunt Karol emerged from the backseat. Skye set off on a slow jog to catch her aunt up in a hug. "Why are you here? Does Mom know you're coming?"

"Maybe. If she thought to look." Karol flashed a grin. "But I don't think she did."

Antonio Alvaro unfurled his tall frame from the car and offered his hand to his daughter, Leticia, helping her out of the car. John Paul followed closely behind his sister.

"This is amazing. You're all here. Welcome to the

Inn of the Three Butterflies." Skye hugged each in turn.

"What a surprise!" Kay squealed from the porch, answering Skye's earlier question.

She barreled down the stairs and hollered, "Mike! Karol's here! Come on out!"

Kay wrapped her sister in her arms. "Why didn't you let me know you were coming?"

"Honestly, until two nights ago I didn't know myself. I want to introduce you to my fiancé, Antonio."

"What? Are you kidding?" Kay's eyes filled with tears. "You're engaged? That's wonderful." She let go of Karol and threw her arms around Antonio. "Congratulations. I'm so happy to meet you."

"The pleasure is mine," Antonio said. "This is my daughter Leticia and my son John Paul. It looks like you have a beautiful establishment here." He gazed at the façade of the inn.

"Thank you. It's been in our family for generations." Kay clapped her hands together. "Let's get some champagne and celebrate. I want to hear everything."

Kay and Karol linked their arms and strolled toward the inn. Four wiggly dogs trailed them.

The driver opened the limo's trunk. John Paul, Antonio, and Mike sauntered over to the car to help unload the bags.

Mike laughed gazing at the mounting pile of luggage. "How long are you staying?"

Skye grabbed a small suitcase and headed to the porch with Leticia. The rumble a motor sounded from behind her. She lugged the suitcase up onto the porch and then spun around catching sight of Gabe's Audi braking next to the limo.

He exited the car flashing her a dazzling smile that speared Skye with a jolt of pure pleasure. Gabe strode over to the men and lent a hand unloading luggage. He grabbed the handles of two large Pullmans and joined Mike, Antonio, and John Paul carrying loads.

Skye scampered down the front porch stairs and intercepted Gabe. He set down the suitcases on the lawn, wrapped an arm around her waist, and pulled her close softly kissing her cheek. The touch of his lips and his musky scent sparked familiar desire.

Mike caught her eye. He widened his eyes and arched his eyebrows cuing her to introduce Gabe.

"Oh…" she stammered. "Dad, this Gabe Hartley. Gabe, my dad, Mike Layton."

Gabe returned Mike's offered handshake. "It's a pleasure to meet you, sir."

"Call me Mike, Gabe. I've looked forward to meeting the man who is dating my favorite daughter." His sea blue eyes sparkled with amusement.

Skye grinned. "He calls each of my sisters his favorite daughter, too."

Mike shrugged his shoulders, beamed at Gabe, and didn't retract a word—he never did.

Gabe continued to help carry the bags into the inn and up to the assigned rooms. Skye headed to the back of the house assuming she'd find her mother scurrying around the kitchen preparing to feed her guests.

As expected, Kay and Karol worked shoulder to shoulder setting out a cold lunch. By the time the men came down to the kitchen, Kay, Karol, and Skye had filled the table with platters of assorted cheeses, meats, and bite-sized pieces of crusty bread.

"Gabe. Come downstairs with me to the wine

cellar?" Dad said. "It's time to break out the champagne."

"Sure, Mike."

Mike and Gabe returned from their mission cradling two bottles of Veuve Cliquot each in the crooks of their arms. The two men were deep in conversation. Skye's attention perked up trying to hear what they said, but she could only make out dual baritones and occasional bursts of laughter. She figured laughter was a good sign.

Kay had filled four ice buckets and set them out on the broad countertop. Mike asked Gabe to put his bottles in the buckets and then popped the corks in the two he had brought up from the cellar.

Mom touched Skye's shoulder and bent her head to whisper in Skye's ear, "I think you make a beautiful couple."

Skye's heart swelled at Gabe's ease with her family. This had to be her destiny. He was meant to be hers.

****

Gabe drifted over to Skye focused on the woman who was the mirror image of Karol, unmistakably Skye's mother and testimony to how beautifully his lady would age.

"Mom, this is Gabe Hartley. Gabe, my mom, Kay."

"This is a pleasure," he said extending his hand to her.

Kay went in for a hug instead. "We hug in this house."

Gabe winked at Skye over her mom's head.

Mike handed out filled glasses of bubbling champagne. He clicked the side of his glass with a spoon. "I would like to propose a toast. To Karol and Antonio. May your lives together be filled with love and laughter. Welcome to the family Antonio, John Paul, and Leticia. There is nothing better than a growing family. Slainté."

Glasses were raised, and each made a point of clinking flutes with the others before taking a sip. The group filed around the buffet, filled their plates, and then drifted to places at the table chatting and creating a homey din of overlapping conversations.

Kay filled her plate last, as usual, and then sat down next to the vacant seat saved for her next to Karol. She leaned forward in her chair as if she couldn't contain her curiosity. "Okay, now tell us all about the engagement. Don't leave out a thing."

Gabe leaned back in his seat, shoulder to shoulder with Skye. He linked his fingers with hers and held her warm, silky hand against his thigh under the table feeling completely at ease in her home with that group of people.

"Three weeks ago, Antonio asked me to marry him," Karol said.

"For the seventh time, I might add," Antonio interjected.

Karol chuckled, patting Antonio's hand. "Yes, you were persistent, my darling. For the first time, I didn't turn him down right away. He had a business trip to Madrid scheduled. We sat and talked for hours the night before he left, and I told him everything in my heart…"

She paused and shot a look at Kay and then at Skye who slowly widened their eyes nodding. Gabe didn't understand the subtext, but unmistakably, Karol had sent some sort of message with that poignant gaze.

211

"…everything he needed to know about me," Karol continued. "Then, I asked him to think about what I had said, and if he was still sure that I was the woman he wanted, he should propose again when he came home."

Antonio groaned. "That was the longest business trip of my life. I was supposed to be gone three weeks and was able to cut it down to two. I had to tell Karol she is all I've ever wanted in a wife." He raised her hand to his lips and kissed each knuckle one by one. "I went straight to her house from the airport."

Karol nodded. "The doorbell rang. The girls went crazy barking. I could swear I heard music," she said, a dreamy expression on her face. "I opened the door and Antonio was down on one knee with an open ring box in his palm."

Tears brimmed in Karol's eyes. "How could I have ever turned down this beautiful man?"

Kay twisted to hug Karol in her chair letting out a little sob.

****

Joyful tears welled in Skye's eyes. *This is huge. Antonio can love Aunt Karol despite the legend?* Hope ballooned in her heart, and she regarded Gabe's handsome profile with new eyes.

Leticia popped up out of her seat and retrieved the box of tissues on the counter. She plucked out a tissue dabbing beneath her eyes and passed the box around the table. "We're a weepy bunch. You won't believe the ring. Show them Karol?"

Karol held out her hand displaying a diamond encrusted butterfly set on an eternity band that caught the light in dazzling sparkles. "He gets me."

"I'd say he gets *all* of us," Skye quipped.

"I have never seen a more perfect engagement ring." Kay shoved her chair back, rose from her seat, rounded the table, and wrapped her arms around Antonio's shoulders. "Welcome to this crazy family."

"Have you set a date yet?" Skye said.

"We have. Tomorrow."

Kay's jaw dropped. "What?"

"As soon as I said yes, Antonio wanted to run to Vegas, but that's not what I had always envisioned."

"I didn't want to give her a chance to change her mind," he said spurring a chorus of laughter.

"I always dreamed of my wedding on our beach."

"Here? Tomorrow? How in the world will I...?" Kay's shoulders slumped, a dazed expression on her face.

Karol touched Kay's arm. "Don't worry, sweetie. As soon as I told Antonio about my dream wedding, he and Leticia shot into action. He chartered the plane; Leticia booked the rooms and the Outer Banks caterer. Everything's set from flowers to food. You don't have to do a thing. Antonio even convinced Fr. Chuck to come out of retirement to marry us."

"Anything for you, my love." Antonio rose from his chair and kissed the crown of Karol's head. "Now I must go and organize unpacking."

"Don't unpack the luggage in my room, darling," Karol directed, as she stood up and tossed her napkin on the table. "It's bad luck for you to see my wedding dress."

"I'll come help you, Karol. It's not bad luck for me," Kay said.

"I'll clean up here, Mom."

"No, darling. You and Gabe go enjoy yourselves.

We can clean up later."

"I've got it, Kay," Mike said. "No problem."

The room cleared in seconds. Gabe had never let go of Skye's hand, eating his meal one-handed. She loved the warm connection to him. She loved everything about Gabe. He gently towed her to her feet. "Would you like to walk on the beach?"

"I'd love to."

Lemony sunshine turned the sand golden; a refreshing breeze cooled her skin, and lazy waves lapped against the shore. Strolling beyond the fringe of seaside homes, Skye and Gabe sat on the firm sand near the water's edge in a secluded spot.

"Alone at last." Gabe moved in for a kiss.

She closed her eyes as his lips melded with hers banishing every thought from Skye's mind. That thrall, the fire that ignited deep in her core was dizzying—urgent. Her entire body leaned toward him, yearning, pulsing with desire. Despite her inexperience, she instinctively knew that making love with Gabe would be perfection. What would it be like to surrender and not constantly overthink the risk? Aunt Karol had found happiness at last, why couldn't she? Was it time to reveal all to Gabe?

He ended the kiss, wrapped an arm around her back, and drew her closer. She rested her head on his shoulder and gazed at the ocean while the ebb and flow of waves doused her toes and sucked at her feet slowly burying them in the sand.

"I hoped that we could have a little more alone time with my parents this weekend. Are you disappointed at Aunt Karol's taking over the inn?" she said.

"Not really, although I'm all for being alone with you. I kind of enjoy all the family chaos growing up an only child. The only thing missing is your sisters."

"They're going to be so mad that they aren't here for this wedding. I'll have to take videos for them."

"I'm fond of your whole family already. I know I'll feel the same way about your sisters."

Contentment filled Skye like a warm embrace. She may not fit into his family, but Gabe fit perfectly with hers.

She took her head off his shoulder and looked into his eyes. His penetrating gaze held hers as he moved to bridge the gap between their lips until he was only a breath away.

Chapter 22

A wet ball plopped into Gabe's lap. His head snapped up. *Talk about killing the mood.* He burst out laughing at the sight of Karol's dogs tearing toward him in a race to fetch.

John Paul was knee-deep in the tide. He cupped his hands at the sides of his mouth and hollered, "Sorry!"

"Nice arm," Gabe yelled back. He stood up and gave a boost to Skye as John Paul let loose with a throw. Another sodden ball lobbed their way.

Skye and Gabe played fetch with the dogs. About ten tosses into the game, the worn-out terriers simply quit and lay down in front of them.

"Looks like our little chaperones are pooped," he said.

"Okay, up," she commanded. "They need a good washing for the sake of Mom's clean floors."

The dogs obediently followed Gabe and Skye back to the inn. Mike was out on the deck tending two grills. The tangy smell of BBQ made Gabe's stomach rumble.

"I'll help your dad." Gabe bounded up the wooden stairs.

Skye turned on the spigot at the side of the deck to wash the dogs.

"Hey, Gabe," Mike said. "Did you have a nice walk?"

"We did, thanks. It's a beautiful stretch of beach."

"That it is."

"What can I do to help?"

Mike handed him a pair of tongs. "Keep an eye on those vegetables? They're Skye's favorite."

Gabe pitched in, glad to help with her meal. "No problem." He turned the skewers and then lowered the lid on the grill.

Mike hung a beefy arm over his shoulder and handed him a bottle of beer.

"Thanks," Gabe said. He clinked the bottle against Mike's and gulped a refreshing mouthful.

Skye caught his eye. She was grinning from ear to ear and gave him a nod.

He grinned back at her knowing how important her father's approval was to Skye. It meant a great deal to Gabe, too.

"I now pronounce you man and wife. You may kiss your beautiful bride." Fr. Chuck closed his Bible.

Antonio swept Karol into his arms for the first, passionate kiss as a married couple.

Gabe joined in applauding and cheering the bride and groom.

Karol clasped her new husband's hand, tore off toward the water, and bounded straight into the waves, tuxedo and bridal veil be damned. The couple's spontaneity was like the shot of a starting pistol. Skye, Gabe, and the wedding guests raced into the water, too, ruining hairdos, makeup, and formal wear in boisterous abandon.

Sloshing out of the water in dripping clothes, Gabe appreciated the way Skye's dress clung to her breasts and thighs. Even soaking wet with her hair plastered to her head, she looked ravishing.

Stripping off the loaner tux from Antonio in his

cottage, Gabe figured he'd offer to pay for a replacement. There was no salvaging the suit.

After changing into dry clothes, the party resumed in earnest beneath a canopy on the inn's grounds.

"This is a feast." Gabe popped a tempura shrimp into his mouth deciding he was too full for another. "I'm done eating. How about you?"

Skye took a sip of her wine and then set her glass down on the table. "I'm stuffed," she said. "Want to go for a walk? I don't think we'll be missed."

"Sure." He crooked his arm, and she slipped her hand over his bicep.

"We can watch the moon rise and be back in time to eat that amazing wedding cake." Skye gave a nod at the three-tiered confection at the front of the tent. "I know the perfect spot."

He held her hand and set off down the beach away from the music and revelers.

"Weddings seem to be our thing," he said.

She turned her face toward him, and her eyes locked on his. Gabe was mesmerized by the expression on her flawless face, the soft surrender in her shining jade eyes.

Much more than physical desire swamped him. He loved her. Only her. *Their* wedding could be their next thing.

She broke eye contact and chatted happily, unaware of the unprecedented feelings swirling inside him. "Antonio did a wonderful job with all the plans. Aunt Karol looked ecstatic."

He joined in the spirit of the conversation. "Best wedding I ever crashed. I wonder how he staged that butterfly's landing on the Bible right in the middle of the ceremony. Butterflies obviously have special meaning to your family with the inn's name and your aunt's engagement ring. That was amazing."

****

"I don't think even Antonio could have planned *that*." Skye squeezed Gabe's hand. *But Aunt Kamille certainly could.*

She had suspected that Kamille would find a way to be with her sister on her special day, despite the birth of her first grandchild at almost the exact time of the wedding ceremony.

Skye pointed to a weathered, wooden bench at the base of a mountainous sand dune. "Here's the perfect place to watch the moonrise."

Gabe and Skye slogged through the sand up to the bench and sat down facing the water. He stretched his arm around Skye's shoulders and drew her close. She nestled against him tucked within his radiating warmth and magnetism, relishing the sense of completion and rightness in his company. Skye and Gabe. A couple. Soulmates. Maybe? If so, she couldn't hope for more.

She focused on the horizon where a bright glow heralded the impending moonrise. "This should be spectacular," she said, still gazing out over the ocean. "There's a red full moon tonight."

"Mmhmm." He undraped his arm from her shoulder and gently massaged the back of her neck sending a torrent of delicious chills through her body.

Skye felt the heat of his gaze on the side of her head, and she peered at him out of the corner of her eye.

He gazed at her profile intently.

"Hey," she said. "You're supposed to be watching for the moon."

"Mmhmm," he repeated as he trailed soft kisses up her neck and along her cheek to her ear lobe.

His hand moved lightly up and down the side of her arm. He continued to kiss the side of her neck and she leaned toward his insistent lips almost abandoning her vigil overwhelmed by the desire he stoked.

But the moon obeyed heavenly order despite Gabe's avid distraction and rose like a scene from *Joe Versus the Volcano*, a butter-colored orb that unfurled a path of sparkling diamonds along the ocean's surface.

"Oh," she gasped. "How beautiful!"

"Yes," he said gazing intently at Skye instead of heavenward. "Beautiful."

"Gabe…"

His lips crushed her mouth, and she met the sensuous assault dead-on, sinking, floating, melting. Gabe's hands skimmed under the back of her shirt and pressed against her shoulder blades flattening her breasts against his firm chest. She necklaced her arms around his shoulders and squeezed him close, her lips still fused to his.

Now he slipped his hands out from under her shirt and laced his fingers in her hair, holding her head exactly where he wanted to devour her mouth, tongues entangling. Skye's body ignited with an urgent desire for total completion despite her innocence. She loved this man with her whole heart, why not her whole body?

He lessened the torrid pressure of his lips on hers and then ended the kiss on a soft moan, his hands still threaded in her hair. His eyes darkened, and he clenched his jaw as if yanking on the reins of galloping passion. "Ah…"

Gabe dipped his head and then raised his eyes to gaze into Skye's. "I want you. More than I've ever wanted any woman."

"I…" She heaved a sigh. "I want you, too. So much."

"Then…" He cupped her face in his hands and moved to kiss her.

Skye shifted away, and Gabe halted with a slight jerk of his head. He knit his brow and gazed directly into her eyes. The expression on his face left no doubt that her fickle behavior had him stumped.

Guilt pierced her. She didn't blame him if he thought she was playing games. How could she reconcile the seesaw emotions warring inside her? Just tell him all her truth? Skye never played games, especially with someone she loved.

She'd start with a partial truth. Skye gently touched the side of his face and then folded her hands in her lap feeling awkward and ridiculously inexperienced. Where was her hot sister, Summer when she needed her?

"I'm a virgin, Gabe. I don't know what to do with these feelings I have for you."

His eyes widened. "Ah," he said with a slight nod of his head. "Darling, I'd *never* rush you or pressure you. Are you, um…"?

"Saving myself for marriage?" she interjected.

I wish it were that simple.

"No, not really. I just have to be…sure."

He took both her hands in his and kissed her palms one by one. "I'm in love you, Skye. I'm absolutely sure about that."

Hearing those words again brought a burst of elation.

She stared directly into his eyes hoping that he could see straight through to the heart he completely owned. "I love you, too, Gabe. I believe I always will."

"Oh, my darling." He wrapped her in his arms and kissed her slowly, thoroughly, scrambling her thoughts and dissolving any lingering doubt.

When he ended the kiss, she saw stars in her eyes. She lay a hand on his warm, muscled arm and bowed her head gathering her wits. What should she say now? Should she ask him what's next? Did he envision a life together with her? If yes, should she spring the whole legend thing and her role in it on him that minute? Was she insane contemplating trusting a public figure with generations of protected secrets? *Not to mention that his mother probably hates me.*

First things first. "Your mother hates me, Gabe."

"She…"

"How could we have a future together?" she interrupted him. "Um, do you even want a future with me?"

Amusement danced in his brown eyes. "No and yes."

Skye did a double take. "What does that mean?"

He gave her a crooked grin. "No, my mother doesn't hate you. And yes, I want a future with you.

"Actually…" he folded his arms and leaned back on the bench. "Maybe Father Chuck hasn't left yet. I'll ask your dad for your hand, speak with the good Father who surely would agree to officiate, and we'll elope right here on Outer Banks."

She elbowed his side. "Now you're making fun of me."

He burst out laughing and draped an arm over her

shoulder. "Truthfully, I love you enough to actually follow through on all that."

Gabe planted a soft kiss on her cheek. "But I want you to trust that I would never hurt you or allow my job to come between us. And I won't ask you to change a single thing. I'm not looking for a politician's wife. I've already found everything I'm looking for. You."

Skye's mind raced debating how to reveal all to Gabe so they might freely pursue a future. How could she survive the heartbreak if he couldn't accept her truth? Regardless, she'd have to think of a way to tell him everything. Because she loved him too much not to try.

What if I slip the new inn brochure into his bag before he leaves? Some place where he's sure to notice it. That helped Bree with Jack and Summer with Vinnie. Well...sort of. I think I'll start with that.

Convinced her plan had merit, Skye rose from the bench, faced Gabe, and held out her hand. "Come on, my love. Let's go back to the inn."

"Sure."

"Your little cottage at the inn."

He didn't move off his seat. "Are you sure? I don't want you to have any regrets with me. Ever."

Love for and attraction to this man filled her near to bursting. "Let's go back. I won't have a single regret."

He shot to his feet and clasped her hand.

Filled with joy, Skye began strolling with him down the beach.

"Skye?"

She turned her head toward him. "Yes?"

"I think I'd like us to jog."

On a laugh she squeezed his hand tightly and set off on a run.

Chapter 23

Skye waited for Bree and Summer at the bottom of the staircase, tapping her foot in a staccato of nervous energy. She had heard Bree throwing up during the night, and right then Skye felt queasy enough to vomit herself. Jitters had her tangled up inside as if a fist had hold of her stomach and *squeezed.* Why had she ever volunteered to be the spokesperson for her group?

Even though her sisters had arrived yesterday to provide her with moral support and strategic advice, Skye knew that she alone would face officialdom to make their case against seismic testing. Bree, Summer, and Skye had brainstormed her presentation throughout yesterday afternoon, during last night, and into that early morning. The triplets had collapsed onto their girlhood twin beds only a few short hours ago.

Slipping her cell phone out of her purse she checked it again for any messages hoping that word from Gabe would soothe and distract her. Nothing yet today. During the past two weeks his schedule had made it impossible for him to return to the Outer Banks and hadn't given him spare moments to contact her except for romantic little "miss you" texts that wished her good-night or good-morning.

Her cheeks flamed at the memory of their intimacy in the cottage. She didn't regret one minute, and she trusted the genuine love they had shared, but their virtual separation unsettled her.

Summer stomped down the stairs, her cell phone nestled between her ear and her shoulder, lugging a bulging briefcase and an armful of folders.

"I'll tell her, Jake. Thanks for all your help. I will." She hooted a laugh. "Really, Jake? Have you met me? At least I know who I can call if I need bail money."

Skye could hear Jacob Levant's hearty laughter through the phone. She had always thought that Jake, her sister's law partner, had a crush on Summer, but it never went anywhere. Summer thought of him only as a brother, and she was crazy in love with her fiancé, Vinnie.

"Jake sends his love and emailed a few more articles we can review on the bus. He wants you to know if you need anything just call him." Summer put her briefcase down on the floor and stuck her phone in its side pocket.

"Thank you so much, Summer. I honestly couldn't do this without you."

Bree hurried down the stairs. "I'm so sorry I'm late. It was a tough night."

"I heard you up a couple of times," Skye said. "Do you think you should stay here and rest? We have a three-hour ride ahead of us."

"No. I'm good. Honest. It's the strangest thing. I have midnight sickness instead of morning sickness. I barf almost every night." She rubbed circles on her bulging belly. "But it's so worth it."

Skye gazed at her glowing sister.

"Let's go kick some bureaucratic ass." Summer led the way out the front door.

Skye drove the short distance to the group's meeting site listening to Bree's and Summer's non-stop pep talk. A mixture of anticipation and dread roiled inside, and she vehemently wished that her public speaking was over...successfully over.

Their coach idled in the parking lot at Jennette's Pier. The triplets boarded the bus where a party atmosphere prevailed. Bonney passed around Tupperware containers of her delicious, secret-recipe, chocolate chip cookies while her husband, Tim, trailed her, handing out large, insulated cups of coffee.

Bonney held two containers of cookies in front of Skye. "Boy or girl?"

Skye furrowed her brow. "What?"

Bonney belted out her signature belly laugh. "With nuts or without?"

"Well of course, boy for me. I always pick one with nuts." She winked at Bonney amid laughter from her travel mates.

The long drive to the State Capitol Building in Raleigh began. Bree dozed and Summer buried her head in a book. Skye shuffled through the note cards of talking points that she and Summer had written last night. She didn't need to memorize the information; it was all etched on her heart.

Skye had envisioned the place where she would battle to stop seismic testing. As she entered the designated room in the government building, she realized that she had seen the meeting site down to the last detail. Rows of folding chairs with blue seat cushions positioned next to and behind a podium with a microphone stand where she would address the committee. A long table draped with red and blue linen, the state colors, headed the room. The table was flanked by the United States and North Carolina flags.

Microphones dotted the tabletop marking the places for the officials who would face her, weigh her words, and determine whether she would win her battle. She shuddered as another bout of nerves gripped her.

Skye's group found seats together in the rapidly filling audience. Glad for the physical nearness of her comrades-in-arms, Skye sat between Bree and Summer, faced forward, and tried to tamp down her mounting anxiety.

The governor and her aides entered the room followed by a few members of the press.

Governor Mary Jordan stood behind the table and looked out at the audience. "Thank you all for taking time out of your busy schedules to join us today to share your concerns about seismic testing along our beautiful coastline. You are not alone. My disapproval is on record with the Administration, and I promise I will continue to support preventing this in every way that I can."

A chorus of boos arose from the back of the room.

The governor wagged her head. "Calm down," she said. "The purpose of this meeting is to share information. I realize both sides are passionate in their beliefs. I only ask you all to be kind today.

"A representative from the U.S. Senate's Committee on Energy and Resources is scheduled to join us but has been detained in traffic. We are recording these proceedings, so we may begin without him. Now, let's get started."

She took her seat. One of her aides consulted a clipboard and called Skye's name.

Skye stood on shaky legs and stepped up onto the podium, her note cards clenched tightly in her hand.

She glanced at Summer, seated on the aisle directly next to her and was emboldened by her sister's encouraging thumbs up.

"Good morning. Thank you, Governor Jordan, for hosting this hearing and for joining in our opposition to seismic testing off the coast of the Outer Banks. My name is Skye Layton. My family has lived on the coast for generations. I have been asked to speak for N.E.S.T., Seal Rescue, and all the other wildlife preservation organizations in my area.

"Seismic testing has caused catastrophic impacts to the marine ecosystem causing injury or—"

The door at the rear of the room closed with a loud boom. Skye turned around at the rude interruption. Her heart somersaulted.

Summer leaned towards her. "Who is that cutie?" She waggled her eyebrows. "Please sit next to me."

"That's Gabe."

"Gabe? Your Gabe?" Summer nudged Bree in the ribs and gave a head nod in Gabe's direction.

"Oh, my goodness," Bree said. "He's a serious hunk, Skye."

"What is he doing here?" Skye wracked her brain for any mention Gabe might have made that his full schedule included attending hearings on this all-important issue.

He's on the Energy and Resources Committee? I really should pay more attention.

Her spirits soared. Surely the man she loved was her most powerful ally in this battle. He knew how deeply she cared about marine life. Now she couldn't wait to continue making her case.

"Please accept my apologies for the interruption,"

Gabe said striding to the head table with a young woman scurrying behind him. "Traffic."

He and his assistant took the two empty seats at the head table. Skye's eyes remained glued to his handsome face. Her confidence that she might succeed in her mission grew with Gabe in the room.

"Folks, this is Senator Gabriel Hartley," Governor Jordan said. "We just started the meeting, Senator. Miss Layton, please continue."

Gabe's focus snapped to Skye's position on the podium. His eyes met hers, and a sexy smile curled his lips. "Miss Layton, you have my full attention."

His formality had Skye biting back a grin. "I was saying, Senator Hartley, that seismic testing has caused catastrophic impacts to the marine ecosystem, causing injury or death to hundreds, if not thousands of whales, dolphins, and sea turtles. For those of you who do not know, seismic testing involves blasting the sea floor with high powered air guns every ten seconds. These blasts disturb, injure, and kill marine wildlife."

Her heart beat wildly, and her body filled with pain at the fate of "her" beautiful animals in the wake of seismic tests. She paused to regain her composure.

"The blasts," she continued, "which reach more than two hundred and fifty decibels, can be heard for miles, can cause hearing loss, and disturbs essential behaviors like feeding and breeding. The noise masks communications between individual whales and dolphins. The blasts have also been proven to reduce the catch rates of commercial fishing—"

"Miss Layton," Gabe interrupted, his eyes on his phone screen. "I believe that the Bureau of Ocean Energy Management describes the technology as, quote, state-of-the-art, computer mapping systems."

He placed the phone down on the table and then looked directly at Skye.

What is he doing? Her role was to present facts, not debate anyone. Especially, not Gabe.

Flustered, she cleared her throat and regrouped. "Actually, Senator, seismic testing is a blunt-force weapon introduced in the 1920s. It was augmented by computer starting in the 1950s. I repeat, it is a *weapon.*

"In addition to the damage testing for oil deposits causes, if deposits are located, offshore drilling expands, and this creates a higher risk for oil spills, more polluted beaches and waters, and fewer pristine places for wildlife and people. In my opinion, there is no good reason to be subjecting the ocean life to these deadly blasts. We need to fight any legislation to allow this testing off our shores. Thank you for listening to our concerns."

Skye turned away from the microphone ready to take her seat.

Gabe's voice boomed stopping her in her tracks. "Just one more question, Miss Layton."

She faced him, trepidation setting her nerves on edge at the sight of Gabe referring to his phone once again. "Yes?"

"Companies hired by the oil industry have stated they have not seen any impact to marine mammals."

Skye narrowed her eyes to slits. "I didn't hear a question, Senator."

"I'm asking for your reaction to that statement." He put his phone face down on the table in front of him.

Skye collected her thoughts and took a deep breath to dispel her frustration with his putting her on the defense. "A marine veterinarian in Peru performed necropsies on dolphins after an unexplained beaching event. His team found that the dolphins examined were bleeding in their middle ears and had suffered fractures there. They had gas in their internal organs and severe pulmonary emphysema, symptoms consistent with death from decompression sickness. His findings concluded the animals had died from decompression sickness caused by acoustic trauma. So, my reaction to your statement is the oil industry will say anything to continue to make billions of dollars at the expense of the beautiful marine life off our coasts. I hope that answered your non-question."

He sat back in his chair as if pleased with her performance.

I'm so confused.

Gabe's phone vibrated. He glanced at the screen and color seemed to drain from his face.

"I beg your pardon," he said, a somber expression on his face. "Governor, may I please have a word?"

Gabe rose from his seat and pulled out the governor's chair for her. They stepped away from the table and huddled in the far corner of the room. He handed her his phone, and she turned her attention to the screen. Her cheeks flamed crimson as she shoved the phone back into Gabe's hand.

She stomped back to her position at the table but didn't sit down. "I'm afraid, the senator has news to share. Senator, please read the message you showed me."

Gabe's pained expression scared Skye. Sorrow? Regret? She gripped the microphone stand, her knuckles white.

"I received a text from my office in Washington." He looked directly at Skye. "I know how committed you all are to protect the coasts and to prevent seismic testing, but I just received word that the Senate passed a bill a half hour ago to allow seismic testing to proceed."

"No," Skye whispered, rooted to the spot, shaking with disbelief.

Chaos erupted in the audience. Both shouts of protests and victory cheers rang in Skye's ears.

****

A single tear slowly slid down Skye's flushed cheek as she stared at him. Gabe's heart twisted like a pretzel. He would do anything to take back the last few minutes.

"Skye, I didn't know," he addressed her as if she were the only person in the room. To him, she was.

Her soulful, jade eyes radiated pain—pain that he indirectly had caused.

"You didn't know that this hearing was a sham, and that Congress was going to pass this legislation anyway? I find that hard to believe. You let me stand here and make a fool of myself."

The accusation of duplicity stung much more coming from her lips. She regarded him with contempt, and he wanted to rush to her, wrap her in his arms and assure her of his innocence. What the hell had happened in Washington to put him in this position?

Skye's chest heaved as she spit out, "You even questioned me, *Senator*, knowing full well it made no difference to you how I answered. I will never forgive you."

In a flash, she fled the room. A pair of doppelgänger women, obviously her sisters, zipped out of the room behind her.

Governor Jordan took the mic. "Please, everyone, stay calm. It's not over. We can continue to fight. This isn't law yet."

Gabe skirted the table and snaked through the mulling crowd.

"Wait. Can I have a word before you go?" the governor called out.

He stopped and turned toward her. "I'm sorry, Mary. I have something more important to take care of now. I'll be back."

Finally, he nudged his way through the rear door, strode through the corridors out to the main lobby, and stood outside on the sidewalk. He scanned the area desperate to find Skye to explain. He was just as shocked as she that the bill went through. Gabe hoped she knew that he had only debated with her because he had known she would have the facts at her disposal. He was asked to bring any information he gleaned from the various hearings he had attended along the Eastern seaboard straight to the Oval Office. Gabe fully intended to do just that as soon as he made things right with Skye.

He spotted her sisters standing next to a bus in the parking lot and sprinted over to them.

"Thank God, I caught you. I need to speak to Skye. Is she on the bus?"

"Skye's not talking to anyone right now." The spitting image of Skye, except for short, chopped hair, crossed her arms across her chest and glared at him defiantly.

Gabe held out his hand. "I'm sorry that we're introduced under these difficult circumstances. I'm

Gabe, and I'm in love with your sister. And you're Summer, I believe."

Summer ignored the offer of a handshake letting Gabe's hand hang in midair.

Bree stepped in front of Summer and shook his hand instead.

He noted her baby bump. "And you're Bree. Skye is beyond excited about becoming an aunt. I'm sure Skye has mentioned me to you?"

"What our sister has or has not told us is none of your business." Summer's sharp tone left no doubt that the Layton sisters were collectively pissed at him.

Gabe knocked on the bus door. "Can you open the door please?"

The driver looked over his head. Gabe turned and witnessed Summer shaking her head, no. The driver stared out the front windshield ignoring Gabe completely.

"This isn't fair," he said. "I just need a few minutes with Skye."

"Fair?" Summer said. "*Fair?* Do you think it was fair for you to embarrass my sister in front of the governor and a packed room? Skye does *not* want to speak to you, Senator Hartley. And trust me; you will not speak with my sister today."

Gabe knew better than to protest further. He wouldn't win this fight with Skye's warrior sister. He hoped he might have a better chance at winning the fight in the Oval Office. Gabe resolved to sway the President to his side so that he might win the day for Skye, after all.

"I'll leave," he said. "But please tell her that I'll make this right in Washington."

"Yeah right," Summer snapped.

Bree placed her hand gently on his arm. "I'll tell her, Senator."

"Please call me Gabe." He looked directly into Bree's pine green eyes, so like Skye's.

"Gabe. It's good to meet you. I'm sorry…"

He covered her hand with his. "No need to apologize."

The driver opened the door with a swish. "Ladies. Time to leave."

"See you soon, Bree and Summer," he said. *I hope.*

He turned away and headed back to talk with Mary.

Chapter 24

Skye had watched his exchange with her sisters from behind the bus's darkened window. She fantasized running to him, making happy introductions to her beloved sisters, and melding him into her family. A useless fantasy. How could she trust a *politician* who obviously spoke out of both sides of his mouth? Or trust him with the legend's secrets? Unthinkable.

She didn't know how to contain the anger swirling inside at the callousness of bureaucrats and Gabe's part in this disaster.

Bree, followed by Summer, boarded the bus and headed straight for her. Bree sat in the aisle seat next to Skye. Summer kneeled on the seat in front of her facing her sisters.

"Sweetie, are you okay?" Summer said.

"Not even close." Skye heaved a sigh. "It all went down the drain from the minute Gabe walked in the door."

She blew out an exasperated breath wagging her head. "And here I thought his appearance meant victory for the coalition. What an idiot I am."

"No, no," Bree soothed. "You're not an idiot at all! Gabe said that he would make this right in Washington."

"He's full of shit," Summer said. "Political double talk, that's all."

Skye huffed. "Not impressed with him, huh, Sis?

237

Sounds like you're as mad at him as I am."

"He sounded sincere, honey," Bree said. "He even said he was in love with you when he introduced himself. That really impressed me."

"Oh, yeah, he's impressive, all right," Skye sneered. "If I weren't so…furious with him, I'd cry."

Summer reached over the seat back and gently patted Skye's hand. "You stay mad, sweetie. He deserves it. I won't let you cry over a man."

Skye slumped in her seat. The fight suddenly seeped out of her and all she felt was defeated. "He's not just any man, Summer. I thought he was the love of my life. And now…"

Skye was helpless to stem the tears that brimmed and streamed down her cheeks.

Summer pursed her lips frowning. "Oh, Skye, please don't cry."

Bree wrapped an arm around Skye's shoulder. "You get it out, sweetie. It will be all right. I just know it."

The next day, for the first time in memory, Skye's eyes were dry when she hugged Bree and Summer goodbye. Maybe she had cried out her reservoir of tears mourning her ruined relationship with Gabe. Or maybe she needed time alone on her beach with her treasured sea animals before their world turned ugly more than she needed sister time.

She immersed in that world every day that week shedding her human form to swim and cavort in the waves, all the while wracking her brain for some way to lead the turtles and dolphins and all the sea fauna to some haven where the devastation of seismic tests couldn't reach them.

When she was on land, she ignored the myriad of texts and emails and voicemails from Gabe, deleting every word without reading them or listening to them. She wasn't ready to confront him and might never be ready. The minute she was forced to witness the havoc at his and his counterparts' hands seemed to mark the point of no return for her and Gabe.

She missed him intensely feeling hollow and depressed that she might never trust him again. How could someone like her possibly make a life with a man without unconditional trust?

Mike and Kay hovered near, silent but ever available. Skye didn't seek out Kay's insights. She was afraid to receive affirmation of the animal holocaust her mother might "see". Skye ignored spending time in her studio except for frequently fixating on her painting of a wildly stormy sea that sat on an easel there. She thought she understood what now seemed the prophetic inspiration for the painting. It represented her entire frame of mind.

That morning Mike whipped closed a newspaper and slapped it down on the table next to his plate when Skye drifted into the kitchen.

"Good morning, love," he said shoving back his chair and then striding toward her.

She accepted his warm hug and narrowed her eyes, focusing on the newspaper over his shoulder. The second he released her she stepped over to the table and picked up the paper.

"Skye, I don't think you should…" Mike said lamely. "The paper is a few days old. I'm just getting around to reading it."

"It's okay, Dad. Whatever it is, thanks for trying to

shield me."

It didn't take her long to find the headline that had prompted Mike's attempt at sparing her bad news.

Boats Outfitted With Air Gun Rigs Dock At South Marina

Skye's stomach sank as she skimmed the article that predicted the President would sign the Energy Exploration Bill within the week. Equipment was at the ready. And seismic testing would proceed. She checked the date on the newspaper noting with alarm that she had little time to save the OBX habitats. How? No matter how fiercely she tried to harness the power of the Sacred Source she couldn't reconfigure nature's rhythms and change migration and nesting patterns. But…

She handed the paper back to Mike and kissed him on the cheek. "I've got to go," she said, already in motion.

"Wait. Where?"

"To the marina," she said over her shoulder.

"Want me to go with you?" he called after her.

"No, thanks. I've got this."

****

Gabe approached the front door of the Inn of the Three Butterflies bursting with good news, but petrified Skye wouldn't agree to hear him out. He had called at least twenty times since the veto two days ago, and she hadn't answered nor contacted him. She should have been elated by the voicemail messages he had left.

Delivering the news in person remained his only course of action. As he waited for an answer to the doorbell ring, he vehemently hoped that she wouldn't reject him despite his delivering against the promise of making things right for her in Washington. So much more than a political victory was at stake. Gabe knew that Skye was the key to his happy future. Without her, no professional win had meaning.

The door swung open, and Mike's brawny form filled the door frame. "Oh boy," Mike said.

"Not exactly the greeting I hoped for, Mike. Hi. Is Skye home?"

"Sorry, son. Welcome." Mike shook his head. "No, she left a little while ago."

He moved to the side and swept his arm in front of him. "Would you like to come in?"

"I'd really like to go find her if you don't mind. Can you tell me where she is?"

"I'd like you to come in for a minute or two," Mike said.

Gabe furrowed his brow, his frustration growing. But his innate politeness and respect for her father had him agreeing. "All right. Thanks."

He entered the cozy parlor and trailed Mike, unbidden, through the house to the kitchen.

"Have a seat," Mike said. "Coffee or something to drink?"

"No, thanks. I'm good."

Mike took a seat opposite Gabe and propped his forearms on the table. His penetrating icy gaze had Gabe on high alert. "I'm not so sure Skye would welcome your visit. Does she know you were coming?"

"She does if she's listened to my last voicemail message. I take it she hasn't."

"Not so far as I know."

"Where is she, sir?"

"Well…" Mike slid a folded newspaper across the

table to Gabe. "She's on her way to the South Marina hellbent after she read this."

Mike jabbed his index finger on the paper pointing to a headline.

Gabe read the print and then looked Mike in the eye. "I don't understand. This is old news. They may have already removed the air gun rigs. I'm not sure. President Lyndon vetoed the bill two days ago."

"Well, *that's* great news." Mike sat back in his chair beaming at Gabe. "You have anything to do with that?"

"Yeah." Gabe grinned. "A fair amount. Do you think it's enough for Skye to forgive me?"

"Should be, son." He twisted his lips. "Then again…she's pretty riled up. And no one has dared utter your name in her presence since she came back from Raleigh."

"She *has* to forgive me," Gabe said. "I'm in love with your daughter, Mike. As a matter of fact…"

Gabe hadn't planned the next thing he said, but in that moment, he knew he was right. "Sir, I plan to ask her to marry me. May I have your blessing?"

Mike chuckled as he outstretched his right arm across the table toward Gabe offering a handshake.

Gabe shook Mike's hand vigorously. "Is that a yes?"

"Son, you've got guts," he said. "Yes. If my daughter accepts your proposal, you have my and her mother's blessing."

Mike got up from the table, and Gabe rose to his feet facing him.

"Thank you, Mike. I'm going to go find her."

"Good. There's no telling what Skye had in mind

when she bolted out of here. Need directions to the marina?"

"I'll find it. GPS."

****

Buoyed by Mike's encouragement, Gabe broke speed limits driving to South Marina, the sun glare through his windshield like a blinding floodlight in his eyes. He parked and then sprinted toward the water noticing Skye's Jeep in a space as he sped past.

Her lithe form appeared as a blur ahead of him. She poised on the end of the dock, where, yes, the boats equipped with seismic testing rigs still bobbed in their moorings. Beyond the horseshoe-shaped sea wall, waves rolled beneath a cloudless, powder blue sky.

She raised both arms overhead rotating her torso round and round, her crimson hair flying wildly. A pie of charcoal clouds appeared directly above the marina, swirling, gathering in sync with Skye's motions. Gabe's jaw dropped, and he stopped in his tracks.

****

The power flowed within and through her as if Skye were a lightning rod for the might of the Sacred Source. She looked up at the threatening clouds that she had fashioned. Satisfied that she had stirred the forces above her enough, she held her arms out directly in front of her and willed the calm sea to froth and roil setting the boats in the marina bobbing chaotically against their moorings. She closed her eyes and threw her head back while she moved her hand as if she held an invisible brush to paint her storm again, this time in nature.

Skye didn't feel guilty about unleashing this fury, although she should have. Kay had drummed the mantra, only for good, into her and her sisters since they were babies. And the Sisters of the Legend before Skye, Bree, and Summer…and backwards through all the generations. Only for good.

She had limited her powers and had respected "the rules", up until today. But now Skye would know no limits in destroying the threat to the creatures she held so dear.

The boats hadn't yet capsized in the wake of her conjured tsunami. On impulse she dove off the end of the dock, speared deep into the water, bound the spell, and then reversed the downward trajectory. The mammoth whale's body that she inhabited would work well as a battering ram.

Skye broke the surface in a freight-train rush of speed and momentum ready to arch sideways and deal a one hundred fifty ton crushing blow to as many vessels in the marina that she could.

"Skye, stop! It's over! No testing! Stop!"

She heard Gabe's voice screaming the miraculous message clearly enough to divert her barrage and submerge harmlessly away from the boats. The water blanketed her from immediately facing two truths: one joyful, the other terrifying. Gabe had somehow made good on his vow to make things right in Washington, *and* Gabe had called a whale by her first name. He knew. *What do I do?*

Skye was tempted to stay underwater…forever. But even in that body, that wasn't an option. She needed air. She also desperately needed Gabe to understand everything about her. As she headed for the surface, she prayed with her whole heart that he might embrace the truth she had just unwittingly and dramatically revealed…and love her anyway.

Chapter 25

Gabe stood helplessly at the edge of the dock scanning the surface of the now perfectly calm water which mirrored the blue sky—not a cloud in sight over the marina.

Did she drown? How could she drown? Whales don't drown.

He widened his eyes and shook his head back and forth scarcely believing what he had seen with his own eyes. Every rumor and story about the Inn of the Three Butterflies he had heard through the years was fact. Skye was magnificent.

Gabe deeply feared that he'd never get the chance to tell her, though, remembering how she'd run away from him when he got too close the first time at Mermaid Cottage. Now he knew why.

"Hi, Gabe."

The sweet sound of her voice brought a rush of relief. He lowered his eyes and found her treading water a foot away from where he stood.

"Thank God," he said. "Come on up here or I'm going to jump in there with you."

"Wh…Why?" she stuttered.

Her baffled expression amused him. "I'd think you might want to thank me properly."

Her eyebrows shot up. "I do…want to thank you…but…"

Gabe extended his arm toward her. "Then, let me

give you a hand."

She swam closer to the dock and held her hand up out of the water. Her deer in the headlights eyes and her maroon hair slicked back away from her face magnified her tender beauty. His lady was indescribably one of a kind.

Gabe squatted down, clasped her hand, and easily towed her out of the water straight into his arms. She trembled within his embrace, and he kissed her crown tasting salty sea water on his lips.

"Skye, you're magnificent."

She gaped up at him. "I…but I…but you…"

He grinned at her. "Yes, you did. And yes, I did. It was pretty awesome."

Almost palpable waves of disbelief emanated off her as she shivered within his loose embrace. "I don't understand. You're not surprised? Hell, you're not shocked to the core?"

"Maybe a little." He nibbled the delicate skin on the side of her neck.

Skye cupped his face with her soft hands and gazed deeply into his eyes. "Gabe don't play with me. This is too important. How can you possibly accept what you just saw…what I've kept secret from you since we met?"

"My sweet Skye, I've known about the legend for years. I just didn't think it was a *real* thing until today."

"How?"

"How did I know?"

"*Yes*! Please. How did you know?"

"I've read, what is it now, three brochures about a legend which made today pretty clear in retrospect. A whale? Wow, Skye. I'm amazed at what you can do. I thought it was all about butterflies."

She snorted a laugh. "And you can accept this? Just like that."

"Why shouldn't I? It's who you are. I love you, Skye. All of you."

She threw her head back and burst out laughing with unfettered glee. "Oh my God, Gabe. I love you, too. I just never thought…"

He couldn't resist diving in to cover her lips with his and smother any remaining doubts. She responded with unbridled passion, the electricity flowing between them like a live wire. Her body melded to his, and he lost all sense of place enraptured by this magical, enchanting woman. Skye encircled his neck with her arms, and Gabe placed a hand on the small of her back pressing her closer, wanting her with increasing ferocity. She ended the kiss on a sigh, her teeth chattering.

"You're freezing. Come on, let's go get you warm."

Skye leaned against him and circled her arm around his waist as they ambled together to his parking space. He opened the passenger door for her. She slipped into the leather seat, and he swung the door closed. Gabe skirted the bumper, opened the trunk, and grabbed a blanket for her just in case the car wasn't already warm enough to banish her chill.

It was about eighty degrees inside the Audi, but she accepted the blanket anyway and wrapped it around her shoulders like a shawl.

She gazed at him, her green eyes sparkling. "Tell me. Why no testing? What did you do to stop the bill that the Senate passed? Your Senate."

He chuckled. "Yeah, well if it were my Senate the bill would never have passed. But. I was sent directly by the President on a fact-finding mission about the environmental impact of both seismic testing and offshore drilling off the Atlantic coast. After the bill passed the Senate, there was unanimous bipartisan outcry from every governor of states along the Eastern seaboard. That, coupled with my strongest recommendations after hearing testimonies just like yours, convinced the President to veto the bill."

"You spoke out against it? For me?"

"Hell, yes, for you. And because it was the right thing to do."

Skye leaned toward Gabe and gave him a kiss. "That's probably the nicest thing anyone has ever done for me. I don't know how I could ever thank you enough."

"I do. Don't let my visit to the inn be for nothing."

She knit her brow. "You mean when you met my family?"

Her cheeks flamed. "And when we…?"

"No. I mean my visit today." Gabe clasped both her hands. "When I asked your father for his blessing."

Her mouth hung open. He beamed at her. "He did give me his blessing, by the way. Hmm. There's no way to get down on one knee in this car, but Skye Layton, will you marry me?"

Epilogue

Skye paced from one end of the sunny studio to the other willing the phone to ring. She breathed in the aromas of paint and freshly cut wood, filled with wonder that Gabe had created this place for her.

A whirlwind of wonderful things had happened since Gabe proposed. He had this amazing studio addition built on top of Mermaid Cottage where they would live after they were married in two short weeks.

Gabe wanted to marry Skye as fast as he could. In planning their wedding, Gabe revealed a whole different side of his personality. His mother wanted the wedding at the farm. The wedding would be at the inn. His mother thought it was too soon; he insisted it was not soon enough. She questioned whether Skye was suitable First Lady material; he told her she was his soulmate and would always be his first lady.

Gabe declared to his mother that he couldn't live without Skye. And she got on board. Now she happily planned the wedding with Kay.

If only the phone would ring. She stopped pacing in front of the painting she had worked on all night—the back view of three cherubic toddler girls, sitting on the sand in front of the inn, holding hands.

She answered the call on the first note of ring tone. "Bree, are you okay?"

"I'm fine. I'm just in shock."

"Why?" Skye said, although she already knew the

answer.

"I'm not having girls. We assumed when the first ultrasound confirmed triplets...the legend...you know. Anyway, today was the sex reveal sonogram. I almost passed out when the technician said, 'The boys look great.' "

Skye placed her hand lightly on her abdomen thrilling at what seemed her babies' stirrings beneath her palm. Her eyes drifted to the painting, and she couldn't help grinning.

"You knew, didn't you?' Bree said.

"Not until last night when I started a painting. I knew in my heart I was painting my daughters and not my nieces."

Skye's phone beeped. "Mom and Summer are calling."

"Of course, they are." Bree laughed.

"Let me add them to our call."

A word about the author…

K.M. Daughters is the penname for team writers and sisters, Pat Casiello and Kathie Clare. The penname is dedicated to the memory of their parents, "K"ay and "M"ickey Lynch. K.M. Daughters is an Amazon Best-Selling author of 16 award winning romance genre novels. The "Daughters" are wives, mothers, and grandmothers residing in the Chicago suburbs and on the Outer Banks, North Carolina. Visitors are most welcome at http://www.kmdaughters.com